Red Fern Press

Red Fern Press books may be purchased for educational, business, or sales promotional use.

For more information, please e-mail the marketing department at redfernpressquery@gmail.com.

First Edition

ISBN 978-1-967038-04-6 (Kindle)
ISBN 978-1-967038-22-0 (Paperback)

Families are made in all kinds of ways.
The only thing that matters is love.

Content

Suggestions for Further Reading

On Fire by Steph West (Red Fern Press, 2023)

Newcross by Steph West (Red Fern Press, 2024)

The Third Period, by Steph West

Clean Break, by Steph West

The Pond House

Double Digits Pocket Romance Series

1

The Wedding

Scout stood in the Pond House's blue guest room and ran her polished index finger over the beaded, glittering bodice of her Vera Wang gown. She glanced in the full-length, oval mirror with a smile. She looked exactly the way she'd always envisioned she would on her wedding day.

Her dark hair was swept away from her face into a soft bun at the nape of her neck and her glossy lips were a rich shade of burgundy. It was the same color she'd been wearing the day she ran into Josh and spilled coffee all over his crisp, white dress shirt nearly three years ago at Double Digits' headquarters.

A small chuckle tumbled out of her throat as she turned her hip slightly and allowed the thigh-high slit in her full satin dress to reveal her smooth, tanned leg and silver Louboutin strappy heels. Josh would like the sexiness of the slit, and the way the strapless corset bodice hugged her curves. She ran her fingers over the sparkling sweetheart neckline and admired the way her breasts looked as they stretched the seams to their limits.

"You look perfect."

Scout turned at the male voice and grinned. "Thank you, Ben."

"You're welcome," he said. He snapped his fingers in approval as he shut the door behind him and stood for a moment to admire her.

"Are those my flowers?" she asked. Her eyes watered a little at the beautiful lavender roses from the property's garden out back. They were cushioned by an ensemble of cream, white, green, and silver flowers in the full bouquet that was tied with a cream-colored ribbon.

"Don't cry, honey, your make-up," he said quickly. He jumped into action, grabbing a tissue from his pocket, and dabbing at her eyes. "And yes, they are."

He smiled as he handed the fragrant flowers to her. She sniffled her tears back into her eyes as she gave him a bright, white smile.

"They're beautiful," she whispered.

"Just like you." He gave her arm a little squeeze. "It's time for Josh to see you."

"Okay." She was breathless and excited as Ben led her from the elegant bedroom down the long hallway toward the front door. Josh had asked specifically for this moment. In his words, it went something like, "I don't wanna lose my shit in front of everyone." In her words, she knew Josh meant that the moment of seeing each other for the first time before they got married was for them and them alone.

She wanted that moment to be private, too. And Ben had taken that direction perfectly, setting up this reveal just as they had requested.

In fact, Ben had done a wonderful job planning their wedding overall, especially since he'd done much of it while she and Josh were still in California, and Ben was here in Pittsburgh. It wasn't until they'd gotten back just after the holidays that she'd spent time with him to get these May nuptials off the ground.

But Ben had done it, perfectly and effortlessly. He'd brought their vision to life.

And now, the day had arrived and, as Josh had promised, the property was in full bloom with sprays of gorgeous flowers and trees everywhere the eye could see.

"You've never seen anything like it, Scout," he had said. "It's just stunning."

And Josh didn't have to say it, but Josh's late mother, Anastasia, was here, too. Her ashes were spread by the pond. Scout knew it was important to Josh to feel his mother's presence today.

"Are you ready?" Ben asked.

She glanced at him with a nod as he opened the front door and yelled to Josh to turn around. Her heart flipped. She had no doubts about marrying him. They would face tough times, she knew that, but they'd find a way to work through it, together. In her heart, from the day she'd met him, it had only ever been Josh.

"Let's go, honey," Ben said. He took her hand and helped her out the door, leading her to the stone path from the front of the house down to the pond. She knew Josh was smiling even though his back was turned to her, his black tuxedo perfectly fitting his muscular, athletic build. His dark hair perfectly in place. She knew he'd be shaved and smell like sandalwood and vanilla.

"Okay, stop here," Ben said as he pointed to the stone steps at her feet.

He took care with fluffing the smooth cream satin and laying it out properly around her. He made sure her hair was in place and the bodice was clean.

"Teeth," he ordered. She showed him her pearly whites. "You got a little smudge. Wipe."

She ran her tongue over the fronts and smiled again.

"Good." He nodded. He moved the dress so her slit was visible and lifted her bust so her breasts were on full display. He gave one last once over and smiled. "Okay, Josh. Count to ten, then turn around."

With that, Ben gave her arm one last squeeze then headed back to the house. It was just the two of them now. No photographer. No families. No friends. No wedding planner. Just her and Josh.

The butterflies tumbled around in her stomach as she felt the tears start to prick the backs of her eyes. She loved this man. Loved him more than anyone or anything in her life. She wanted to give him everything—herself, a home, a family, a beautiful life. She swallowed quickly just as he started to turn.

Children. A flash of doubt hit her in the gut. The doctor said it was possible, even with endometriosis in the fallopian tubes like hers, to get pregnant—but it was a longshot. Their fertility specialist said they'd need to try for at least six months and then they could come back and address any issues with her and the doctor. Scout had the next full year off due to her non-compete, so they'd started trying two months ago just in case, and to no avail. Not yet anyway.

Maybe never.

She shook the thought out of her
mind as Josh turned completely
around and the tears fell from his
eyes, then hers.

"Scout," he whispered. He
stepped to her and gripped her
waist. She could barely breathe as
she gazed into his rich, dark eyes.
She reached up and touch his
perfectly coifed dark hair, then
touched his bow tie as the tears slid
down her face.

"I love you," she choked out.

"I love you, too." He wiped his
eyes then pulled her in and gave
her a light kiss. He smiled as he
gazed longingly at her. "I've
imagined this moment since the
day I met you."

He used his thumbs to wipe
away her tears.

"Me, too," she whispered.

"You're beautiful," he said.

"Thank you. You, too."

His gaze turned sultry. "That slit in your dress is fire, baby."

She couldn't help but laugh and he happily joined her.

"You should see what else is underneath this dress," she teased.

"Oh, baby," he said. "I can't wait."

They laughed as he pulled her to his body and wrapped his arms around her. "I'm so excited to marry you."

"Me too, baby." She let out a small exhale.

"And someday, a family, however it comes to us," he whispered in her ear.

She nodded into his shoulder and knew that he meant that. Josh loved her, and whether they had a baby or not, would never change that.

But it mattered to her. She wanted to give him a child. They weren't even married, and she could feel that pressure, that desire, pulsing inside of her.

And she knew in her gut that it wouldn't be Josh she'd have to reconcile her condition or their future with—it was going to be with herself.

And she hoped she could do that without hurting him or their relationship along the way.

2

The Red Devil

A year and a half later

Scout couldn't quite be sure if the rush of tears streaming down her face as she sat on the commode in their spacious sage and cream-colored bathroom were from the Clomid or the blood on her underwear.

"Damn it." She sobbed into her hands quietly so as not to wake Josh. They had now been trying to get pregnant for nineteen months with no hint of anything working. At least she had Buster in this moment, who used his cold snout to nudge her hands as he licked her arms.

"Thanks, buddy," she said tearfully as she used one hand to pet the four-year-old golden retriever and the other to cover her sobs.

For the first six months of trying to conceive, they did all the fun stuff—sex everywhere, all the time, and in every different position imaginable. The Kama Sutra had been their best friend and she had fancied all the adventurous lovemaking. She had never felt so alive or sexy in her life then having Josh slide his hands down her slick, sweaty body and move her into new positions at his will that hit her G-spot just right.

"Josh," she had moaned repeatedly as he thrust inside her and filled her time and again.

"God, Scout," he had panted. And they had enjoyed each other passionately in ways they'd never done with anyone else.

But six months became seven and they found themselves seated in the doctor's office, their fertility specialist in tow, asking why they still weren't pregnant.

"Let's try some lifestyle changes," the medical professionals had said. "And track your ovulation."

And after another few months of nothing happening it was Eastern medicine they recommended, including a stint of acupuncture. "Like Charlotte in Sex and the City," Scout had whispered to Josh.

Then it was Clomid medication, which de-escalated her estrogen production to help stimulate hormones that could help her conceive, but which, to-date, had only made her have horrendous mood swings, sore breasts, and other symptoms that mimicked pregnancy but without pregnancy.

And now this. Her period. Again. And it was getting harder and harder to walk out into the bedroom on these mornings and face Josh with the news. Again.

Her chest heaved as she sobbed into her hands and Buster retreated. She flinched when she felt Josh's hands on her shoulders and lifted her face to see him kneeling in front of her.

"Oh, I didn't mean to wake you—"

"Scout." He wiped her tears
away and gave her a light kiss as
warmth and love emanated from
his stare. "The red Devil, huh?"

She nodded and the hot tears
poured down her face as he pulled
her into him.

She sobbed on his shoulder as
her arms gripped him tightly, but
after a while, she realized his baby
blue T-shirt was soaked wet with
her tears and snot. Her eyes had to
be puffy and swollen.

"I'm sorry, Josh," she
whimpered as she pulled away.
"I'm sorry I can't get pregnant."

He stood up, grabbed a box of
tissues from the porcelain cream-
colored sink and brought it back,
handing it to her. She took it and

wiped her face with a tissue, then blew her nose.

He knelt in front of her again as he used his thumbs to wipe away the remaining wetness under her eyes.

"Baby, getting pregnant or not getting pregnant is not going to define us," he said quietly. He grinned. "I married you because I love you. I can't live without you. You make my life. My whole life. And that doesn't change whether we have a baby or not."

"I know, but," she started, then paused.

"Please tell me you're not doing all this stuff to your body only for me, Scout," he said.

She gazed into his dark eyes and could see he was worried. He loved her. It wouldn't matter. But it did matter to her because that made her want to give him a baby even more.

"I'm not," she said. That was mostly true. She did want a baby. She wasn't sure she wanted it more than Josh. And she wasn't sure she wanted it in any way possible. That was the thing that weighed on her mind.

She wanted to get pregnant naturally. It had been a stretch for her to move to taking Clomid. And for the last few months they'd been talking about invasive or alternative things like freezing her eggs, surrogacy, IVF, or Intrauterine Insemination. They'd also put their application in for adoption in the months just before they got married. At the time, Scout had done it as a back-up plan. Now it was looking like it could be their actual plan she wasn't entirely sure she was ready for it.

But Josh was. He was inclined to adopt over such invasive methods to get pregnant. It wasn't just that he didn't want her to go through it, he also believed strongly in the concept of giving a child a home.

And she hadn't made up her mind just yet.

"Scout, baby, we can stop trying anytime," he said. He brushed his finger across her cheek, and she leaned into his sweet gesture as they locked eyes. "This is so hard on your body. The Clomid. All of it. It's like, all the pressure is on your body. I'm not loving it, you know?"

"I know," she said quietly.

"I just want you," he said. "Maybe we should take a break, huh?"

To hear him say it was a relief. She did want to take a break. Then she looked in his eyes and all she could think was that there was a baby for them, and that baby had his beautiful, soulful dark brown eyes. And it ate her up all over again that she couldn't give that baby to him.

"Okay," she said tearfully. She nodded and wiped away the tears. "Maybe just take a month or two off."

He nodded. "Yeah."

She exhaled a small breath as she felt the weight of their situation lift. At least for this month, she could relax. "Let me clean up and then I'll make breakfast."

"Are you crazy?" he asked. He leaned in and kissed her then stood up. "I'm gonna walk Buster, then make *you* breakfast, baby. Pancakes, bacon, fruit, and coffee."

She glanced at him with surprise.

"Yeah I know, we were limiting coffee and caffeine," he waved his hand as he walked to the door. "Not today. Today, we enjoy our life together. Are you gonna be okay to go to Zach's birthday party?"

It hit her in the chest when he asked. She had briefly forgotten about Zach's second birthday party. It was hard to believe Lucas and Jaime's son was already two and Casey was four. And today was

Zach's actual birthday and the party. October third. There would be babies and children and pregnant moms everywhere.

And she wouldn't be one of them.

"I'm okay," she said. She felt the hot tears hit the backs of her eyes.

"Scout," he whispered. He started to walk back but she put up her hand to stop him.

"No, Josh, it's okay. I'm okay. This is for Jaime and Lucas, and we love those kids," she said quietly. She wiped at her eyes and took a deep breath. She exhaled slowly. "We're the best aunt and uncle those kids have. We can't disappoint."

"Yes, we can."

An emotional moment passed between them as she nodded, and the tears rolled down her cheeks.

"I'll be okay, Josh, I promise."

He nodded as he walked over and kissed her once more. "I love you."

"I love you, too," she said. He wiped her eyes again, kissed her, and walked out.

She felt the tears rise again and she quickly ran to the door and closed it quietly before covering her face and mouth and sobbing into her hands once more.

Josh grinned as Jaime grabbed Scout the minute they walked into Lucas and Jaime's home and stole her over to the birthday boy as Lucas walked up and slapped him on the shoulder.

"I can't believe he's two already," Lucas exclaimed.

"Hey man." Josh leaned over and gave his younger brother a quick hug in the stunning white, blue, and stainless-steel kitchen. "I can't believe how fast he's growing up. It's like just yesterday we were holding him in the hospital."

"I know, right?" Lucas said. "You look like hell, man."

"Rough morning," Josh said. He put his hands on his hips and exhaled slowly as Lucas eyed him.

"What?" Josh asked. He crossed his arms over his black polo and gave Lucas a look.

"Why was it a rough morning?" Lucas asked. He took a swig of his beer, his yellow shirt making his sandy-colored hair look more blonde than brown. "What's goin' on?"

Josh let out a sigh as he watched Scout hold a blonde-haired, blue-eyed Zach, sticky from candy and cookies, and give him kisses. It hit Josh hard in the gut how badly he wanted a family. But never at the expense of his wife or her feelings or her body. Then again, watching her with Zach, he knew she'd be an amazing mother if given the chance.

"Scout…this morning," Josh said quietly. He looked around to make sure no one was nearby. "We're not pregnant. Again."

"Oh shit," Lucas said. He squeezed Josh's shoulder. "I'm sorry, Josh, really."

"I know," Josh said. He glanced at Lucas. "Listen, don't say anything to Dad or Katherine, okay?"

"Sure, man, no problem," Lucas said. "Just…"

"What?" Josh asked. He looked his brother over and could see Lucas was itching to say something. "Lucas?"

"I cannot think of a worse time to tell you this," Lucas said. He shook his head and glanced at his feet, then back to Josh. "Jaime's pregnant."

"Oh," Josh said. He knew what their good news was going to do to Scout, but he also didn't want to deny his brother's happiness. "Hey, man, it's all good. I'm so happy for you two."

Josh gave his brother a hug then stepped away.

"Thanks, man," Lucas said. He took another pull of his beer. "We're excited."

"You should be," Josh said. "That's…you guys have a great little family. I'm excited for you."

"It's coming for you, too, Josh."

Josh shrugged and sighed. He peered at his brother. "I need a beer, brother."

"Yep." Lucas walked to the cooler and grabbed a cold one. "So, changing subjects, is Scout ready to start back as the CEO of Double Digits on Monday?"

Lucas grabbed a towel and wiped the bottle dry as he walked back to Josh.

"Ready? She's been ready since she left three years ago." Josh laughed. "She was born ready for this job."

"She's gonna kill it, man," Lucas said. He twisted off the beer cap and handed the bottle to Josh.

"She really is," Josh said. He took a long swig and reveled in the ice-cold liquid hitting the back of his dry throat and giving him some relief.

"Are you worried?" Lucas asked.

Josh swallowed the cold beer and glanced questioningly at his brother. "About what?"

"That she'll go back to work, love it, and replace the idea of kids with her career?"

Lucas was the only person in his life he'd let ask him that question. And also, the only person he'd answer honestly about it.

"I am," Josh answered. "But I knew what I was getting when I married her. I know Scout loves her career. And she's damn good at it. I mean, if she were a man, no one would ask her to think any differently. People only question that because she's a woman."

"And what about you? You have needs, too, Josh."

Josh nodded and took another drink of his beer. He swallowed as he thumbed the label then looked at Lucas.

"I want a family," Josh said. "I want what you have. I want…"

He stopped short of saying the thing he really wanted because in the same way Scout felt pressured to have children, he felt pressured to have a career. And that wasn't what he wanted.

"What, Josh? Be honest. It's me, so you can't bullshit me. You know that."

Josh half-laughed, then looked at his brother earnestly.

"I wanna be a stay-at-home dad," Josh said sheepishly. "I wanna, like, do the whole dad thing. Car pools, drop-offs, PTA. All of it."

Lucas laughed. "You get that from mom," Lucas said. "She loved being a mom, you know? You've got that same passion for parenting in you. That doesn't surprise me at all. And you'd be great at it. And you can babysit for us."

"You're an asshole," Josh scoffed. The two brothers laughed as they watched Scout and Jaime with the kids, all the children running around on sugar highs, the moms gathering in small groups and gossiping, the DJ playing children's music and the balloon artist making dogs and horses.

"Does Scout know that's what you want?" Lucas asked.

"God no, not yet," Josh said. He caught Lucas's side eye. "It's not like before. I'm not lying to her. If I told her that right now, it would feel like pressure. And right now, she doesn't need that. She just needs me to love her. And if it happens, it happens. And if it doesn't, I'll do what I've been doing—I'll pour all that devotion into our nonprofit and help the children and families that we do through the Foundation."

"Okay," Lucas nodded. "I support you either way."

"I know you do, thank you."

"Should we go take on the children and the bounce houses?" Lucas asked.

"Maybe one more beer." Josh said.

"Yeah," Lucas nodded. He turned to get the beers, but Josh stopped him.

"Hey, can you maybe tell Jaime to wait to say anything to Scout about the pregnancy? Just…not today."

"Sure, no problem," Lucas said. He pulled his cell phone out of his pocket and texted Jaime. They both glanced out and saw Jaime pull her phone out of her pocket, read the text, then text back. Lucas read it. "All set, man. She'll wait."

"Anyone else know?" Josh asked.

"Nah, not yet," Lucas said. "So, all good."

Lucas slapped Josh's arm and turned away. As Lucas grabbed two more beers, Josh smiled watching Scout bounce Zach in her arms. His heart swelled at the sight. She was everything to him. And he hoped that someday they'd have a little baby that she'd carry around just like that.

If not their own, then maybe a baby they'd adopt who needed a good home and two loving parents.

Josh could only hope Scout would continue to feel the same way.

3

Transitions

Scout parked her white Lexus SUV in the private parking garage of Double Digits and shut it off. She glanced in the rearview mirror and double-checked her hair and make-up. She had taken time this morning to make sure every detail of her look was impeccable. This was it, she was the CEO, the buck stopped with her, and she had to look the part.

Her sleek navy-blue dress fit her curvy body perfectly and her heels were classic and nude. Her dark hair was long and loose, the big curls falling effortlessly below her shoulders. Her lips were burgundy, and her green eyes were bright and clear.

That was a huge shift from the past weekend when she'd cried her eyes out more than a few times. The stress of not getting pregnant had been wearing her down and getting her period again was the proverbial straw.

She let out a slow exhale, grabbed her purse, and hopped out of the car. The clicking of her heels against the pavement was already refilling her soul and making her feel whole again. She had felt it as soon as she'd woken up this morning. There was a brightness in her body that hadn't been there in months. This company was her baby. The place where she knew

she was successful, and Paps had
wanted her all along.

She'd stayed away for the last
twelve months per her non-
compete. In that time, Josh and
Lucas had run it and the
Foundation well together as COO
and CEO. Their strengths and
weaknesses balancing each other
out as she had suspected they
would. Then, once her twelve
months had been up, she started to
slowly give input and take
meetings as Josh transitioned out of
Double Digits and back to the
Foundation while Lucas shifted
into the COO role.

They'd planned for her official
takeover today and had followed
the transition plan to a tee. Scout
had a new assistant, Sophia, since

Belle retired the year before, and she'd already started setting up Scout's meetings for this week.

It had all been exciting and given her something to think about other than getting pregnant. She could feel her whole body relax as she stepped into the private elevator and hit the up button to the C-suite.

She wished Paps could be here for this moment. He had mentored her, believed in her, trusted her, and treated her like his own family.

She grinned to herself. That wise old man had known even then Josh and Scout were perfect for each other. They had set up a photo of Paps and Bessie, as well as Josh's mother, at their wedding, and lit candles in their honor.

The elevator dinged and the doors opened to the C-suite. She grinned as she realized she was the "C" now.

"Good morning, Mrs. Janssen," Sophia said brightly.

Scout stepped powerfully out of the elevator and smiled at the blonde-haired, brown-eyed, twenty-something dressed sharply in a smart pencil skirt and white button up.

Scout loved hearing her married name, there was no doubt about that. It was a reminder of her and Josh's love and commitment to each other. But she was her mother's daughter, and she believed in a woman keeping her own bank account, her own assets, and certainly, her own identity.

"It's actually Mrs. Cruz-Janssen."

"My apologies," Sophia said quickly.

"No worries. I kept my own name and added Josh's," Scout said. She stopped in front of Sophia's desk. "So, today is going to be a busy day.

"It really is," Sophia said.

"Walk with me." Scout gave her assistant a nod as she headed toward her office. Well, Pappy's former office.

She walked in and immediately felt at home. It was nearly as she remembered it except for the things she'd done leading up to this day. She changed the blacks to creams, had new carpet installed, got rid of the bar cart, and updated the bathroom to include a nursing station. The thing that remained was the black and white photo of Paps and Bessie on the desk. She smiled at it now as she sat down and turned on her laptop.

"First meeting in an hour with the new designer for our workout line," Scout said.

"Yep, and a staff meeting right after to give your state of the company brief and next steps," said Sophia. "Josh will be there and he's taking you to lunch right after. Then we have meetings with every team this afternoon to set the course."

"Perfect, jumping in feet first," Scout said with a satisfied grin.

"You've been here five minutes and you're already crushing it,"

Lucas said as he walked into her office with a wide grin. He sat down on the cream-colored leather couch and reached to the glass coffee table, then looked around confused. "Where's the candy?"

"You can't be serious," she quipped.

"I am serious, I like my candy," Lucas said. "Paps always had it for me."

Scout grinned as she opened her top drawer, grabbed a box of chewy sweet tarts, and threw it his way.

She glanced at Sophia. "We're good, Sophia. If you can just take one final look at the presentation deck for the state of the company?"

"Right away," Sophia said as she hurriedly left the office.

"Smart assistant," Lucas said. He ripped open the box and tipped it back to his mouth as the pieces slid in. He started chewing. "I might have to poach her."

"Find your own assistant," Scout warned.

Lucas chuckled as he gnawed on the candy. "You look like a natural in that chair. Feels right."

"Thanks." She smiled at Lucas and let out a sigh. "I miss Paps."

"Yeah." Lucas nodded. "Me, too."

"You and Josh did a great job running this place. And before that, you did incredible work. Why are you so willing to give it up, Lucas?"

Lucas shrugged as he stood up and walked to her desk. He ran a finger over the black and white photo.

"Paps and Bessie had a family," Lucas said. "Josh and I…we had the company. And it was like that every day after our mom died. Until Josh met you and I met Jaime. Neither of us want that for our families. Where the company and the work is the only thing our kids see."

"I get it," Scout said. She nodded and looked back to her computer screen.

"I'm sorry about what you and Josh are going through," Lucas said quietly.

"I know," she said. She shot him a weak smile. "Just maybe…can we not talk about it at work?"

"Of course. I get it," he said. "I'll give you time to get ready. You're gonna kick ass today."

"Thank you," she said. He turned and walked out as she glanced at her computer and then the picture of Paps and Bessie.

Scout wasn't sure what she wanted at this point. The hormones and the repeated failure to conceive had left her empty inside. This job filled that void. It felt good to be back and be successful at something. But more than that, she felt like herself again and not just Josh's wife or the wanna-be mother.

Here, at Double Digits, she was in charge. She was in control. And she liked that. She wasn't confined to being a woman or a mother or a wife. She was the boss. And it felt freeing.

She wasn't sure what it meant for her and Josh's future in terms of a family, but for the first time in a long time she was happy to not be talking about her failure as a woman and instead be focused on her success as a leader.

She took a deep breath and exhaled.

Maybe her and Josh didn't need kids at all. Maybe they could be happy just like this.

4

Two Roads

Josh slid on his black oven mitts and carefully took the roasted chicken out of the oven and admired his handiwork. It was browned perfectly and smelled like onions, garlic, and rosemary. He placed it on the counter to rest then turned and added a touch of butter and sour cream to the freshly mashed potatoes before wiping his hands on the black dish towel and throwing it over his shoulder.

"Buster, no!" Josh scolded. The golden retriever wagged his tail and looked eagerly at the chicken. "Nope. Go lay down."

The canine dropped his head and went off to lie in his bed as Josh finished up.

This was the first dinner he and Scout would have together in almost two weeks since she started back at Double Digits, and he wanted it to be perfect. *Needed* it to be perfect.

He walked to the dining room and lit the tapered candles on the sleek, black dining table before adjusting the silverware just so. He lightly turned the delicate white and blue China plates they'd gotten for their wedding and scanned the table settings for any imperfections.

"Excellent," he whispered.

He walked back into the kitchen and checked the time: seven o'clock exactly. Scout should be

home by now. He grabbed the
white Chardonnay and poured
generously into their stemmed wine
glasses, then started to cut the
carrots for sautéing.

Ideally, they'd eat, talk, relax,
and have sex like two people who
wanted to connect and express their
love for each other. It had been
more than two weeks since the last
time they'd made love. After she
started her period, she'd shut him
out. He understood that, but now it
had crossed into territory he was
uncomfortable with. There was too
much distance between them, and it
felt like it was only getting worse.

Scout had been taking meetings
she didn't need to, stayed late at
work for reasons that didn't seem
necessary, and had, more or less,

been avoiding him and their relationship. It was most likely about their pregnancy issues, but he was sore about the fact that he didn't know for sure.

Plus, he still hadn't told her about Jaime being pregnant and he didn't want to hide it from her anymore. They'd been through that during their engagement and it didn't pan out well for either of them. So, while initially he didn't Scout about Jaime to protect her, now it just felt like he was withholding it.

He grabbed the sauté pan and tossed it on the burner, turning up the heat and coating it with olive oil just as his phone rang.

"Hey Dad," Josh said after he hit the answer button and speaker phone. "Make it quick. Scout'll be here any minute."

"Sure," R.J. said. "Just making sure you two are coming to dinner this weekend. Katherine and I are shopping now. Steak good?"

"Sounds great," Josh said. He tossed the carrots into the heated oil, and they sizzled loudly as he grabbed the skillet's handle and gave the vibrant orange veggies a toss. He sprinkled brown sugar over the concoction and tossed it again.

"You cookin'?" R.J. asked.

"I am," Josh said. He smiled as his carrots started to glaze. "I'm pretty damn good at it, too."

"Sounds like it," R.J. said. "Katherine wants to know if you want a sweet potato or a baker."

"Baker," Josh said. He removed the carrots from the heat and dropped them into a blue and white China serving dish, then quickly covered them with foil. "Scout will want the sweet potato."

"Got it," R.J. said. After a pause he added, "So, any grandbaby news?"

"Dad," Josh said with a warning tone.

"Hey, your brother is way ahead of you." R.J. laughed innocently. "What can I say? I can't believe it, but I love being a Papaw. I want some more of those little heathens crawlin' around."

Josh grinned. He knew it was coming from a good place, but if Scout walked in and heard that, or if he told Scout R.J. had said that, it would just make things worse.

"I know, Dad, I know," Josh said. He looked around. Everything was ready. He glanced at the clock: Ten minutes after seven. His forehead wrinkled. "Hey, I'll give you a call tomorrow, okay?"

"Yeah sure, son, talk then."

"Bye."

"Bye."

Josh looked at his phone. No text. No phone call. He walked to the mud room door and opened it, glancing into the garage. No Lexus. He glanced at his watch.

"Where the hell is she?"

Scout glanced at the dashboard of her Lexus as she pulled into the garage and the door shut behind her. It was well after midnight, and she was exhausted. She shut off the car and sat for a moment looking at the door into their home.

It wasn't fair of her to stay this late and not communicate it to Josh. She knew he was making dinner, knew he wanted to talk, knew by his actions that he wanted to have sex.

She didn't have it in her. And she didn't want to tell her husband, who she loved, no. It would hurt him to feel like she didn't want him and that wasn't true—she wanted Josh. She wanted him all the time. But the way she was feeling right now, she wanted to extend it a little bit longer before diving back into the conversations they needed to have.

Right now, Scout was happier than she'd been in about six months. She was back in a place that respected her and wanted her for something other than her ability to make babies. Or rather, her inability. She didn't have to focus on her flaws at Double Digits, she could focus on her successes. She could control them.

And she didn't have to face the conversation she and Josh needed to have about whether having children was even on the table anymore.

"Oh," she uttered involuntarily as tears hit her eyes. The thought of no children with Josh felt like a ton of bricks coming down on top of her. She covered her mouth and shook her head.

No, she wanted children with Josh. But if she couldn't have her own, she didn't know how far she wanted to go to get that dream. That was the question she was asking herself these days: How far was she willing to go and for how long?

The proper answer when you loved someone was to say, "I'll go the distance. As far as I need to."

But the honest answer was that it was hard on her body to go through the constant rigors of trying to get pregnant. The hormones were insufferable, and now they were talking about truly invasive procedures. And the truth was, she

had a career. One that she loved,
with people relying on her for their
jobs and security. And those next
steps would upend her work.

If she was honest with herself,
she just didn't want to have this
conversation with Josh yet because
she didn't know what she wanted to
say. It hadn't become clear in her
mind.

She ran her finger over her
stomach and flinched.

If anything, Scout was likely
leaning more toward adoption than
invasive procedures, but bringing
someone else's child into their
home and not knowing their
background was something to think
about. Yes, those children needed
homes. And she and Josh could
provide that. But the uncertainty of

their backgrounds was a concern. Even more concerning was whether she could love an adopted child like it was her own. What would that feel like?

She sighed as she grabbed her purse and climbed out of her car. She walked to the mud room door and opened it into their home. She immediately saw the dining room table. The candles had been blown out, but it was still set and waiting for her. She wiped the tears from her eyes as she set her purse down and walked into the kitchen. It was perfectly clean with only a note on the counter: *I made you a plate. It's in the fridge. Love you. Josh.*

Her heart skipped in her chest as she realized the lengths he had gone to. She owed him this

conversation. And if their
engagement had taught her
anything, it was that coming to a
conclusion about anything
involving her and Josh was
something she needed to allow Josh
to be part of, instead of trying to
come to a decision on her own.

She smiled. She would take
tomorrow afternoon off, buy some
pretty lingerie, come home, and
love him the way he deserved to be
loved. And then, they could eat
these leftovers and talk this
through.

She owed that to him and to
herself to figure out how they
would proceed from here. And it
was something they needed to do
together.

5

Undecided

Josh woke up to sunlight streaming through their large bedroom windows and his cell phone ringing. He quickly snatched it from the side table of their bed and answered as Buster jumped onto the bed and snuggled next to him.

"This is Josh," he said groggily. He rubbed the soft fur of his canine buddy as he tried to wake up.

"Josh Janssen?" a female voice said.

"Yes, who am I speaking with?" He sat up in the King-sized bed and glanced at Scout's rumpled side where he saw a note on the pillow.

"Off, buddy," he said quietly to Buster, who jumped down and walked out of the bedroom. He reached over and grabbed the note as the woman started to speak.

"This is Brenda with the Sunshine Adoption Agency. You and your wife, Scout, placed an application with us almost two years ago?"

"Oh, yes, yes," Josh said excitedly. Suddenly awake, he jumped up and started pacing across the bedroom, his bare feet smacking against the hardwood floor. "That's us. How can I help? Do you need anything from us?"

The woman laughed at Josh's excitement and he smiled broadly. The timing of this call could not be more perfect. Especially if there was a baby, and it was meant for him and Scout.

"Well, we have a young woman who is pregnant and wants to give her baby up for adoption. She reviewed your application and has narrowed it down to two families and you and Scout are one of them."

"Oh my God," Josh said tearfully as his eyes misted over. He swallowed hard and got it together as he slapped his bare chest to clear himself up. "Yes, we want to interview with her. Please, we'd love to."

"Okay, perfect," Brenda said. "Let me talk with the mother and I'll get back to you within the next couple of days about a time next week or so. Sound good?"

Josh was nodding without saying anything before he finally spit out, "Yes, it's…it's perfect, yes. Thank you. Thank you so much."

"You're welcome, Josh," she said. "I'll be in touch."

"Thank you," he said as they both hung up.

He looked around his room for a minute then threw his arms in the air. "Yes!"

Buster ran in at Josh's excited voice and jumped with him.

"Yes, Buster, yes! You might have a brother! Or a sister!"

He laughed at himself as he remembered Scout's note and took a look: *I'm sorry about last night. Tonight, it's all about you and me. Take off the afternoon from the*

Josh grinned. Finally, Scout was ready to talk, and from the looks of that note, maybe a little bit more. He glanced at his watch: Eight thirty.

"Shit," he hissed. If he was going to take the afternoon off to be with Scout, he needed to get his ass into work.

He tossed his phone and the note on the bed and ran for the shower.

If this was the conversation he thought it was going to be tonight, he'd be able to break the news about Jaime to Scout and follow it up with this fantastic news about a possible adoption. Win-win.

"Yes," he said as he stripped off his blue pajama pants and jumped in the shower.

This was exactly the break he needed to talk to Scout without her being too hurt. And hopefully, after this, they'd be on their way to having a baby of their own.

Scout parked her Lexus in the Foundation parking right next to Josh's black Land Rover. She was going to surprise him at the office and sweep him away to a late lunch then home for a passionate afternoon of sex and talking.

She glanced at the pink bag with hot pink tissue paper and grinned. Josh was going to love the black

lacy number she'd gotten to wear
for him.

"Oh, baby, indeed," she said.
She grabbed her Chanel
pocketbook and stepped out of the
SUV before sashaying through the
parking lot.

"Is that Jaime's car?" She eyed
the back Escalade and saw the car
seats in the backseat. "It *is* Jaime."

Scout smiled as she walked
through the front doors to the
receptionist.

"Scout," Leslie said. She smiled
brightly as her red hair tumbled
elegantly over her shoulders.
"Wow, everyone's here today."

"I know, I saw Jaime's car,"
Scout responded.

"Yeah, she's running the
fundraiser for Children's Hospital,

so she's meeting with her committee right now," Leslie said. "Perfect timing, too, right? Since she's due just after."

Scout froze in place. She heard it, but she couldn't believe it. Jaime was pregnant?

"I'm sorry, did you say due?" Scout asked stunned.

"Yeah, can you believe how perfect the timing is? Baby number three. I hope it's a girl this time. I know that's what Jaime's hoping for."

"Yeah," Scout said. She wasn't sure how to react, so she just smiled and said, "Here's hoping for a little girl."

The swirl of emotions raged inside of Scout's chest. She wanted to cry, and vomit, and throw something, all at the same time. There was no way that Leslie, the receptionist, knew about Jaime's pregnancy and Josh didn't. *Fuck, fuck, fuck.* How could Jaime have three children and she couldn't even have one?

"Is Josh in his office?" Scout squeaked out.

"He is, go right in," Leslie said. This time, her freckled face had lost its smile and was less peppy as she took in Scout's expression and realized she'd said something she shouldn't have.

Scout nodded and swallowed hard as her stilettos clicked down the steel and silver hallway and into Josh's large, warm office. He was on the phone and had his back turned to her as she shut the door with a quiet click. When he finally realized she was there, he turned with a smile. As soon as he saw her face, his smile dropped.

"Hey, Bob, can I call you back in a little bit? Yeah, great, thanks."

He put his phone down and they stared at each other for a second.

"Scout, I was going to tell you tonight."

"How could you keep it from me? How could she?" Scout said, her voice starting to waver.

"What?"

"How could she have another baby and I can't even have one?"

Scout collapsed under the weight of her own failure as Josh caught her on the way down. Yes, why? Why exactly couldn't she give Josh the thing he wanted most? The thing she wanted most? And Jaime was popping them out like there was nothing to it.

"Scout," he said as he gripped her in his arms. "I'm sorry, baby, I'm so sorry."

"I don't understand," she wept.

"I don't, either, baby, but I love you and there are ways…"

"No," she said fiercely. She shoved him away and struggled to stand, grabbing her fallen purse and moving toward the door as Josh stood and faced her.

"What do you mean no?"

"If I can't have a baby, I don't want one. I don't want to keep going through this. This constant failure."

"Scout, wait—"

"No, Josh, you promised me, you said if we couldn't have a baby, if I didn't want it, then you and I would be enough, right? That's what you said, right?"

She searched his face and thought she saw something in it, but as quick as it had come, it was gone.

"If that's what you want, then yes," he said quietly. "We can stop. I did say that. We have each other, our careers, and family. And nephews, and maybe a niece. And that's enough. It really is."

She rushed to Josh's arms and let him hold her as she cried her whole soul out. She wasn't entirely sure she meant everything she just said, but for this moment, it was what she needed. She needed to know it could just be them and that was enough.

"Let's go home, huh?" Josh asked. "I'll make you something to eat and we can talk."

She stepped away and wiped her eyes. She looked at her amazing, gorgeous, wonderful husband and she suddenly felt urges that had been under wraps for the last two weeks.

"I have a better idea of what we can do."

She gave him a weak smile as his widened.

"Yeah, let's do that," he said huskily as he pulled her into his arms and kissed her deeply.

She wasn't sure which emotion was stronger in this moment—her pain or her pleasure. But she knew it was what she needed. She couldn't take any more blows to her confidence. She just needed to feel good in this moment. And it had to be Josh who did it.

She wanted to give her husband everything. And if she couldn't give him a baby right now, she'd give him her love, her body, and everything she had.

And more importantly, she was giving it to herself. She needed this break. This time to just be in love with him again and to not worry about anything except how good they could make each other feel.

And that's exactly what she was going to do.

6

Steam and Dreams

The first hour of lovemaking in their fluffy, white bed was everything Josh needed to connect to his wife again. Feeling her body in his arms, moving inside her, kissing her after the pleasure they both experienced brought them back to the place they were at when they got married.

"Baby, that was amazing," he whispered as he gently kissed her forehead and squeezed her closer to him as they lay side by side in their bed. His heart rate slowly came back to resting as they basked in the afterglow of their afternoon escapade.

"Mmm, Josh, we needed that, baby," she murmured.

"We really did," he said quietly. He slid his fingers gently up and down her back. "I know this has been hard on you, baby. I wish I could change that."

"I know you do."

"I'm sorry I didn't tell you sooner about Jaime."

"I know why you didn't," she said. She glanced up at him with those big, green eyes and perfect lips, red and swollen now from their passionate kisses. "I'm sorry I haven't been coming home for dinner."

"I know," he said. He slowly exhaled. "You didn't want to talk about all of it, right?"

"I still don't," she said quietly.

He nodded. He desperately wanted to talk about it, but he could tell it wasn't what she needed right at this moment.

"Let's not talk then," he said. He looked in her eyes and she smiled.

"Really?" she asked hopefully.

"Really," he said. "How about you let me make you feel like it's our honeymoon all over again."

Her eyes lit up at that remark. "Shower?"

"Shower," he said. "I'll meet you there."

She jumped out of bed and her beautiful naked, curvy body ran into their bathroom suite. He could hear the shower fire up and saw the steam start to drift out the door as he grabbed his phone and sent a quick email to Brenda at the

Sunshine Adoption Agency: *We need a bit more time before we meet with the adoptive mom. Can we have a week?*

He put down his phone. Right now, his wife needed to feel like his wife, his lover, and his partner, not his babymaker.

And that's exactly what he was going to do. He stood and walked to the bathroom where Scout was already in the shower. She peeked out at his approach.

"Come in, baby, it's nice and warm."

He grinned at her and stepped into the warm, steamy water as he touched her slick, wet body.

"Damn, baby," he whispered. "Your body is amazing."

He ran his hands over her
curves, settling for a moment on
her full, heavy breasts, then
reaching around to her backside
and giving her a playful squeeze.

"Josh," she whispered
seductively as she slid her hands up
his back. He pulled her close and
kissed her deeply and with passion.

He gasped when her delicate
hand found his manhood. "Scout,"
he moaned.

He backed her up against the
shower wall and lifted her up as she
wrapped her legs around him. The
steam was swirling around them
now and the water pounded his
back as he moved inside of her.

"Josh," she panted.

This was more like it. This was
the Josh and Scout Josh loved. The

two people who loved and cherished each other and showed it in every way. Sex with his wife was the best sex of his life. It always was. And he would give up a thousand conversations to have these moments with her.

"Scout," he moaned as he thrust deeper inside of her.

"Oh, baby," she gasped. "Don't stop." She pushed against him as his length went deeper and deeper.

Josh could see the pleasure on her face as he slowed down and waited until she looked in his eyes.

"This feel good?" he asked gently. She nodded as she moaned.

"Josh, yes."

He sunk deep inside of her. "You like that?"

"Yes," she said softly. "More,
baby."

He started to thrust a little
harder. "Like this?"

She kissed him then as he thrust
even deeper. A moan of pleasure
erupted in her throat.

"Yes!" She gripped onto him and
pulled him in as her hips thrust
toward him, pulling him deeper
inside her. "Harder!"

Josh lost all control then. Scout
was his weakness. His love and his
lover, the woman he couldn't live
without. The woman he would
choose over anything and anyone.

"I love you, Scout."

"I love you, too, baby."

He could feel her tighten around
him and he tightened, too. As they

both experienced pleasure, they
each started to relax into the other.

"That was perfect," she said.

"It really was," he said. He
kissed her gently and put her down
as they held each other in the
warm, flowing water.

"You and me, baby," he said
quietly. "Forever."

"Yeah," she replied. "Forever."

And in that moment, it felt like
they released all the tension and
worry of whether they would add to
their family. It didn't matter. It
really didn't matter.

They could travel, they could
concentrate on their nephews and
maybe a niece, they could give
back in big ways to their
community. They had plenty of

love and resources to give—and that could be enough.

He kissed Scout and looked in her beautiful, green eyes—eyes he had hoped a child might have someday. And something inside of him clenched tight.

He *hoped* it was enough. But it was certainly enough for now.

7

Dinner with the Family

Scout smiled brightly at the dinner table loaded with food and drinks as R.J. and Katherine told yet another story from their tropical vacation.

"I mean, holy shit, did you know spiders could be that big?" R.J. laughed. His hands were wide and every time he told this tale his hands got a few inches further from each other. Pretty soon, that spider was going to be as big as dog, according to R.J. Scout couldn't help but laugh at him.

"Gotta love the tropics, huh?" Lucas asked. He took a long pull of his wine as he grinned at Jaime in her cute little red sundress and matching sweater.

"Did you guys see any on your honeymoon?" Katherine asked. Katherine always tried to bring everyone into the conversation. Scout just adored her. She was warm and friendly and loving, just like right now, in her tan and cream sweater and tan riding pants and boots. Her hair was long and loose around her face.

"No, thank God," Jaime said. "I'd have died."

She stabbed at her potato and took a big bite. "This is delicious, you guys, thanks for having us."

"Yeah, of course," Katherine said. "We wanted to get everybody together before we put the grill away for the winter."

"Scout, I hear you're kicking ass at work," R.J. said proudly. He turned his attention to her, his eyes bright from the alcohol and good conversation, his button-down open at the chest and his sleeve rolled up. "How is Pap's legacy holding up?"

"Good," Scout said. She put her fork down. "Great, actually. Lucas and Josh did amazing putting it in a good position for me to take it over and now we're already anticipating huge revenue growth with the partnerships we're putting together."

"Well, Paps really believed in you, so, salute," R.J. said. He raised his wine glass, and everyone followed with "Salute."

"Thank you," Scout said.

"On that note," Lucas said. "If we may?" He glanced at Scout and Josh, and they each nodded. Scout had been dreading this moment up until her and Josh decided to take a break. Now, it felt like she could just appreciate their good news and congratulate them earnestly.

Lucas turned to Jaime, "My love."

She laughed as she glanced at R.J. and Katherine. "We're pregnant again."

"Ah!" Katherine screamed as she jumped up with excitement, followed quickly by R.J., as they ran and hugged Lucas and Jaime.

Scout felt Josh squeezer her leg under the table. She glanced to him and smiled as they shared a knowing look. She loved him so much. The break they were taking from talking about everything was helping, but in this moment, she could suddenly tell it wasn't going to be enough. She could feel it inside of her that she wanted a family with him. It was just a matter of how.

As Katherine and R.J. sat down, R.J. looked at Scout. "So, when are we hearing this news from you two?"

"Dad," Josh said sharply.

Scout could feel the heat rising up her throat into her cheeks. "Uh—"

"R.J.," Katherine said as she shook her head. "Forgive him, Scout, he's just really loving the whole grandpa thing."

"Yeah, I'm sorry," R.J. said. "Really. I thought…I guess I thought we could talk about it. I apologize."

"It's okay," Scout said quietly. She knew R.J. didn't mean any harm but it still stung. "Will you excuse me for a moment?"

She slid her chair out and quietly left the table as Josh asked, "Do you want me to come or—"

"No, I just need a minute," she whispered. She gave him a kiss and walked out into the cool night air on the back deck with brightly lit tiki torches. She pulled the fresh air into her lungs and felt the tears sting her eyes. What was she going to do? It just all felt so confusing. One minute she was certain she didn't want any kids and the next minute she was crying because she couldn't. Her hormones, her thoughts, her mind was all over the place.

"Can I join you?"

Scout turned to see Jaime. Jaime was the last person she wanted to see right at this moment. But maybe she was the exact person Scout needed.

8

Sisters

Scout gave Jaime a light smile as her sister-in-law's blonde hair moved lightly in the wind. "Sure, you can join me. Though, I'm probably not good company, unfortunately."

Jaime gave a weak smile back. "I'm sure I'm the last person you want to see."

"I'm sorry if I've given you that impression, Jaime," Scout said sincerely as Jaime walked up and stood beside her. "It's just hard to be around you right now, by no fault of yours at all. I promise, I'm trying."

"You don't have to do that. It won't bother me if you're mad or

sad or whatever you feel," said
Jaime. She crossed her arms across
her chest for warmth. "I get it. I
promise."

Scout and Jaime shared a brief
look. Scout could see the sincerity
in Jaime's eyes, and it hit Scout
right in the gut. She couldn't stop
the tears that flooded her vision as
the sobs erupted from her gut.

"Oh Scout," Jaime said. She put
her arms around Scout's shoulders
as they shook with pain.

"It's okay; I'm okay," Scout
said. She pulled her tears back and
calmed down as Jaime stepped
back but kept rubbing her back for
a moment. "I promise. It just hits
me sometimes. I feel…I feel
broken. You know?"

Jaime nodded emphatically. "I understand." Jaime stopped rubbing Scout's back, then touched her own belly.

"What's it like?" Scout asked. She nodded to Jaime's stomach.

"Wonderful," Jaime said wistfully. "It really is. I mean, hurts like a son-of-a-bitch when they come out."

Scout couldn't stop the laugh that burst from her throat. Jaime laughed with her.

"I've heard that," Scout said. She chuckled as she wiped her eyes and tucked a hair behind her ear.

"But being pregnant, yeah, it's wonderful," Jaime said. "But I've been lucky. Not all women are. Lots of women have pregnancy conditions, lose babies—it happens. So, even getting pregnant, things can still be tough."

Scout nodded. "I just want a shot, you know?" Scout choked up as the words came out.

"Are you going to try IVF?" Jaime asked.

Scout sighed as she wiped the final wetness from under her eyes and looked at Jaime.

"We've talked about it. And Intrauterine Insemination," Scout said. "Plus, adoption."

Jaime nodded. "Lucas had mentioned Josh said that."

"I thought about nothing at all, too," Scout said. "You know, if I can't have Josh's baby, just not having one. I'm all over the damn place." She shrugged.

"Is that what you really want?"
Jaime asked.

Scout shook her head. "I want to
raise a family with Josh. It's really
just a matter of what to do next.
And I'm just…I guess I haven't
decided."

Jaime nodded. "It's your body.
You have to decide your limits."

Scout nodded. "I'd do anything
for Josh. I can try whatever we
need to try. At least once. I think."

"Are you sure?"

"I think so," Scout said. She
sighed. "I don't know. I love him.
More than anything. I owe it to him
and to me and to us, you know?
And Josh…well, he's damn near
perfect, so I know he'll take care of
me through it."

Jaime and Scout laughed loudly.

"Damn near perfect, huh?"
Jaime asked sarcastically.

"I thought I was gonna get away with that one." Scout laughed.

"Not on your life," Jaime asked. "Now, Josh and Lucas *they* think they're perfect."

"Unbelievable, right?"

"Uh-huh," Jaime said as she stroked her stomach. "Look, what's supposed to happen is going to happen. And you two are going to be fine."

"I believe that," Scout said. "Josh and I both believe in meant to be. We always have."

"Good," Jaime said. She gave Scout an encouraging smile. "Should we go back to dinner and shove R.J.'s foot in his mouth?"

"Absolutely," Scout said. They turned and started to walk inside.

"That man is an idiot sometimes," Jaime said.

"Did I ever tell you how he took food off my plate?" Scout asked.

"He did what?"

The women laughed as they headed back to dinner.

9

Brothers

Josh and Lucas shook their heads at each other across the traditional cherry-wood dining table as R.J. and Katherine did the dishes in the roomy kitchen of their spacious five-bedroom home. The gorgeous house was in an upscale Pittsburgh neighborhood about twenty minutes from the Pond House.

Cleaning up the evening's dinner was Katherine's attempt at separating R.J. from his sons, who at this precise moment wanted to kill him.

"Always count on dad to make a stupid comment at the exact wrong moment," Lucas said. He scoffed as he grabbed his half-full wine glass and took a long sip of the rich cabernet.

"You'd think he'd learn over time, but…nope." Josh took a swig of his thick, brown Guinness from a tall beer glass then set it down with a thud as he ran his thumb up and down the side.

"Now that they're busy in the kitchen, though, how are you doing, man? How's things?" Lucas asked. He leaned forward with concern, his forehead wrinkling.

Josh shook his head. "Not good, brother. Not good." Josh leaned forward to and rubbed his temples instead of the glass.

"Are you still trying?"

"I mean, we're still having sex. But Scout quit the Clomid a couple weeks ago. We're not tracking her cycle. We just…stopped everything."

"That all happen after her…you know, monthly friend?" Lucas asked. He chuckled at his own shyness of asking as Josh grinned.

"It's just…it's so much pressure on her," Josh said quietly. He sighed as he sat back in his chair and mindlessly tapped the table.

"It's hard for you, too," Lucas acknowledged. "I mean, not as hard as Scout, it's her body. But, for you, I know how badly you want a family."

Josh glanced at Lucas then away.

"What?" Lucas asked.

"Nothin'," Josh said. He shook his head.

"Don't do that. I'm your brother.
I know you've got something on
your mind. What?"

Josh glanced around to make
sure the coast was clear. "Adoption
agency called," he whispered.

Lucas leaned in and whispered
back. "And?"

"Young mother. Wants to put her
baby up for adoption. She wants to
interview me and Scout."

"Dude, that's amazing." Lucas
tapped the table softly with
excitement.

Josh shrugged then took a chug
of his beer.

"Oh shit, you haven't told Scout
have you?"

Josh shook his head as he put his
beer down.

"You gotta tell her, Josh," Lucas
warned.

"I am, I promise," Josh said.

"Like you were gonna tell her
about Jaime's pregnancy?" Lucas
raised an eyebrow.

"I know, I know," Josh said with
frustration. "I just…I'm trying to
navigate what she can take and
what she can't and I'm not even
sure she wants a family at this
point, let alone adoption. I just…I
want to give her a few days."

"Well, don't wait too long,"
Lucas said. He took a quick sip of
wine. "It's easier for her to deal
with the truth then to not know and
try to make decisions. Plus, it'll
piss her off if she finds out you hid
it."

"I know," Josh said.

Lucas shook his head vigorously at Josh then smiled broadly at someone behind Josh, making him turn to look.

"Hey ladies," Lucas said as Scout and Jaime walked in. "Everything good?"

Josh smiled at Scout and reached out his arm for her to sit on his lap. "You okay, baby?"

"I'm good," she said. She slid onto his legs and draped her arm around his neck. She ran her fingers into his hair and gave it a little tug. "I love you."

"I love you, too," he said. He kissed her back when she dipped down and touched her lips to his. He grinned. "Mmm, tug on my hair again."

"You like that, huh?" she teased. She tugged again.

"Yeah, baby," he said. They both laughed.

"Come here, my love," Lucas said dramatically as he pulled out Jaime's chair. She sat down and gave Lucas a kiss. "Can I get you anything?"

"I'm good," she said. "We should probably get going, though. We only have the babysitter for another forty-five minutes."

"Yeah, let's do it." Lucas and Jaime stood up, then Lucas sat back down again. "Whoop. Maybe had a little too much wine, there."

"Keys," Jaime said. She flipped her hand out with a grin. "I miss wine."

"Sorry, baby," Lucas said as he grabbed his keys from his pocket with a boyish grin.

He lightly tugged on her hand when he dropped his keys in it and gave her a kiss.

"You get a pass tonight because I'm still early," Jaime said.

"Got it, baby." Lucas grinned. He looked at Josh and Scout. "Alright, it was good seeing ya'll. We're gonna head out."

Josh nodded and Scout grinned. "Drive safe, Jaime," Josh said. "Sleep well, Princess."

"I will," Lucas smirked. He pointed at Scout. "I'll see you in the office tomorrow."

"You're ridiculous. Let's go." Jaime laughed as the two headed to the kitchen to say goodbye to R.J. and Katherine.

Josh gave Scout another kiss as he slid his hands around her waist and pulled her tight to him. "You sure you're good?"

"Yeah, I am," Scout said. She ran a finger down his cheek, then pulled him in for another kiss. "But, how about we talk this weekend? Really talk. About everything."

"I'd like that." Josh smiled brightly. She was willing to talk and that's all he could ask for right now. "Ready to go?"

She nodded. "Yeah, baby, I am."

"I'll say goodnight to R.J. and Katherine," he said. He handed her the car keys. "You head out and get comfortable."

"Okay." She nodded. "Tell them I said thank you. And that we're good."

"I will," he said. He patted her hip. "Let's go."

Scout took his keys as she stood then headed out to the car as he headed toward the kitchen.

As much as he appreciated the sex they'd been having, they needed to talk. And he was glad that she was finally in a place for them to do just that.

10

Let the Scheming Begin

Lucas leaned back with warm happiness as he glanced over at Jaime, once, twice, three times, as she drove them home.

"What?" she asked. She glanced at him then back at the road as she adjusted the volume of their oldies but goodies playlist, turning it down. Her blue eyes shined as a passing car's headlights him them just right, her blonde hair glowing under the yellow beams.

"I just love you, that's all," he said.

"Aw," she said. She reached over and squeezed his hand. "I love you, too."

"Thanks for driving, baby," he said.

"Of course," she said. She shrugged as she grinned. "You've done it for me. You'll do it for me again. Especially after the baby comes. Ugh, I can't wait to have wine with dinner again."

They both laughed as they hit a stop light on their way home, which was about ten miles from the Pond House. Josh loved being close to his brother. This was exactly what he was hoping for when he asked them to come back to Pittsburgh.

He felt Jaime's eyes on him and glanced at her as she glanced away quickly.

"What?" he asked. His interest was piqued. He knew his wife. She was up to something.

"What?" she asked back. She shrugged again as she shifted in the leather seat making it crinkle.

"Listen, wifey, I *know* you, I know you're scheming," he said as she laughed. "Now, tell me, so I can get in on it, too."

He turned excitedly to her as she leaned her right elbow on the console and got closer to him. "Okay, here's what I'm thinking."

"I knew it." He snapped his fingers as he nodded at her and sat up, leaning in. "Hit me with it."

"Okay, well, Scout told me, when we were outside, that she's pretty sure she wants to have a family but isn't sure what steps to take next."

"Okay, that tracks," Lucas said. They were putting two and two together now. "Josh got a call from the adoption agency about a possible baby and hasn't told her yet."

"Whaaaaaa?" Jaime drew out the word as she reared back. "What is it with these two and not telling each other things?"

"It's Josh. He's trying to find the right time to tell her. Thinks she's taking things to heart now."

"Well, she probably is. It can't be easy for her. Especially with me being pregnant again."

"True," Lucas said. He reached over and squeezed her thigh lovingly.

"Having said that, any time is the right time to tell the truth," Jaime said. She lightly ran her finger up and down Lucas' arm.

"I know. But you have to understand, with Josh, people have expected him to hide the truth and just go with things. Since mom died. So, his knee-jerk reaction is to hide and protect. He's getting better," Lucas said. He glanced at Jaime who smiled at him then turned back to the road. "So, what do you propose, my wanna-be Lucy?"

"Well, my side-kick Ricky, the best way to know if you want to proceed with kids is to actually have kids."

Lucas glanced at her when she paused and saw her wiggle her eyebrows.

"Oh, you mean our kids?" He laughed as he sat up straight in his seat.

"I do," she said. She grinned.

"Honey, we want them to *want* kids not fear them," Lucas said.

Jaime laughed as they hit another stop light. "Oh, come on, our kids are awesome. Just…adventurous. I believe they're what's called, energetic."

"Sure, baby, let's go with that." Lucas squeezed her leg as they both chuckled and the light turned green. "So, you propose more than a night of babysitting?"

"Yeah, more like a weekend," she said. "Plus, we could use a little time together. Celebrate the baby."

She stroked his arm seductively with her finger.

"Baby, don't you start that, or I'll have you pull this car over now."

"Promise?" she asked. She gave him a wickedly flirtatious smile, then started to pull off the road.

"Baby, no, there could be murderers," he said. "You listen to true crime podcasts all the time, come on now."

She laughed and got back on the road. "Alright, fine. But can I get the good lovin' later since I drove home?"

"Already on my mind, honey," he said.

"And are you gonna go along with my plan?" she asked.

"I've already got the vacation place picked and everything."

"Aww, you're the best, baby," she said. "I'm gonna give you the A+ lovin', too."

"Hot damn," he said as he slapped his hands together. "Let the games begin."

11

Babysitter's Club

Scout tried to suppress the giggle desperately trying to escape the confines of her throat as she stared at Josh, his Calvin Klein shorts, Ralph Lauren polo, and carefully crafted hair that were now thickly covered with spaghetti and peas. Babysitting Casey and Zach had taken a horribly wrong turn, and he was suffering the consequences.

"I feel fairly confident Lucas and Jaime did this on purpose," Josh huffed as he scraped the noodles from his light blue shirt. As if on cue, Casey and Zach laughed wildly at their handiwork. Josh gave them the fatherly eye. "Is this funny?"

The two little boys leaned into each, squirming in their seats as they nodded at Josh and giggled mercilessly.

Josh glanced up to Scout who now had her hand covering her mouth as she watched him.

"Just laugh already," he snarked as he shook his head to get the peas out of his head. They tumbled onto the table eliciting a guffaw from the boys.

Scout laughed with them as she reached over and picked a noodle off his neck then dropped it on his ceramic white plate. "Yes," Scout agreed with him. "I absolutely think this is another one of Jaime's schemes that Lucas went along with."

"Think it's about…you know?" Josh asked. He gave her a slight smile as he pulled the last of the noodles off his pants and dropped them on his plate. He glanced to Casey.

"Not funny," Josh said as seriously as he could.

"Yes, it is Uncle Joshy," Casey said, drawing out his words slowly and with humor. Zach nodded wildly.

Josh tried to hold back his smile, but he couldn't. Casey and Zach were like mirror images of him and Lucas. And it made him love them even more.

"Goofballs," he said. He glanced at Scout who was gazing sweetly at him. "What?"

"You were made to be a dad," she said quietly. She leaned back in her chair and sighed. "And yes, I do think this weekend of babysitting is about us and what we're gong through."

"They're never gonna stop with the scheming, are they?" Josh asked. He grinned.

Scout shook her head. "Doubtful."

"So, they must want us to talk," Josh said. He leaned back, too. "That always seems to be why we end up in the middle of their tangled webs."

"I think that's a reasonable bet."

"Talk!" Casey ordered as Zach laughed.

Scout and Josh chuckled as they eyed the messy boys, who had

more food on them than in their
bellies.

"They are so like me and
Lucas," Josh said nostalgically.
"Brothers."

Scout laughed. "Totally," she
said. They eyed each other for a
second with happy smiles. "How
about we clean up, then take them
for a walk, bath time, and after we
put them to bed, you and I can
talk?"

"If we have any energy left,"
Josh lamented. "Who knew
parenting was this exhausting?"

"If you knew, you might not do
it," she said. She eyed the boys.
"Then again, they're so darn cute, it
really doesn't matter, does it?"

Josh grinned as he eyed his wife
and saw nothing but warmth and

love in her eyes. The way she
stared at the boys and took care of
them. She was a natural at loving
and caring for another person. The
look on her face told him she felt
that, too.

"It doesn't," he said.

"Although, maybe next time, we
don't wear designer clothes, huh?"
She nodded at his destroyed outfit.

He glanced down and laughed as
he pulled at his messy clothing.

"Yeah," he agreed. "Maybe go
with the basics next time."

"Yeah," she nodded. She stood
and started to clear the table.

"Boys, how do you feel about a
nature walk before bath time?"
Josh said excitedly as he clapped
his hands together.

"Yeah!" Casey yelled as he tossed his arms in the air.

Zach gurgled with happiness as he started wiggling wildly.

Josh's heart swelled with joy as he watched them together. He felt a deep desire in his gut to be a father as he stood and grabbed the wet wipes Scout had set out by the spaghetti. A smart move he now appreciated.

He wiped the boys faces first, then their hands, before scrubbing their arms as Scout wiped down the kitchen table.

"Casey, go change your shirt, buddy," he said.

"Okay," Casey said as he raced to his room.

"Your turn," he said to Zach, who reached up his arms for Josh

to pick him up. The move melted
Josh's insides as he picked up the
tiny two-year-old and held him.
"Let's get you a new shirt, too,
buddy."

Scout caught his eye then and he
saw her staring at him with a look
of absolute love and devotion.

"What?" he asked.

"Nothing," she said. She
shrugged and went back to the
table. Then looked back up at him.
"Kids look good on you."

His whole body warmed as they
stared at each other.

"I'm gonna change him," he
said.

"Okay," she said quietly. "I'll
finish up down here.

"Okay," he said.

He walked over and gave her a quick kiss as they shared a moment with Zach firmly between them.

It's exactly the way he wanted to feel for the rest of his life.

And he hoped Scout was starting to feel that way again, too.

12

Bee Sting

As they embarked on their nature walk—which amounted to strolling through the wooded suburban neighborhood on its flower-lined sidewalks—Scout was now the one holding Zach in her arms as Josh walked, and occasionally ran, with Casey who was riding his black and blue dirt bike like a pro.

"Easy buddy," Josh said as Casey swerved into the empty road. "Stay outta the road. Come over here. I need to adjust your helmet."

Casey did as he was told and listened to his Uncle Josh. Scout could tell how much the boys loved him. It wasn't just that Josh was an authority figure they respected, but also that he was a buddy they could have fun with. Josh had the natural ability to get dirty and play like a kid, but also tell them what was what, and they listened.

He was everything she wanted him to be as a father and her gut flinched at the hard truth of what they were going through. She sighed and smiled at Zach who gave her a generous grin. He pointed to the flowers along the sidewalk. "You wanna pick a flower?" she asked.

Zach nodded happily as she put him down. He had walked early, like both Josh and Lucas had, but he was still bobbling a bit as he wobbled over to the flowers.

She glanced quickly to Josh as he finished with Casey's helmet and got him up and running again. It was right about then she heard the buzzing and quickly looked back to where Zach was.

"Zach!" she yelled as she grabbed for him. But it was too late, just as he reached for one of the bright yellow daisies, a bee flew out from behind it and stung him. It elicited a loud scream from the toddler who looked at her with surprise as big, alligator tears pooled in his eyes.

"Oh no," Scout said. She swept him up in her arms and swatted the bee away as she checked the sting for any swelling.

"He okay?" Josh yelled as he and Casey stopped to look at them.

"He seems like it," she said. She watched him closely for a second but didn't see anything happening except that he was starting to calm down. "Hmm, let's get you home and get some anti-sting medication on you, okay?"

He nodded as his tears fell down his face and he stopped waling. She grinned at him as she bounced him with comfort for a moment until he was completely calm. She yelled to Josh, "Hey, let's head back and treat this, okay?"

"Okay," Josh said. "Casey, let's head back." Casey nodded and turned around as they both started back.

Scout kissed Zach's forehead and then panic set in. "Oh my God, Josh."

"What?" he said quickly, turning to her with concern.

"His lips are swelling," she said. Panic rose in her stomach as she watched his lips getting bigger by the second and a wheezing sound starting to come from his throat. "Oh my God, I think we need to call 9-1-1. Is he allergic to bees?"

"Shit, I don't know," Josh said. "Casey, hurry." They all rushed back and into the house as Josh pulled out his phone and called for emergency services. "Hello, yes, we're babysitting, and my nephew is reacting to a bee sting. Swollen lips. Wheezing. He's two. Not sure. Yes, that's the address. Thank you. Yes, we'll try to find an epi pen."

Scout put Zach down on the couch as she assessed his vitals.

"Squad is coming," he said. "Casey, sit down."

"He's having trouble breathing, Josh." She tilted his head back to open up his airway.

Josh was already on the phone to his brother and turned it on speaker mode.

"Dude, this better be—"

"Lucas, shut up. Is Zach allergic to bees?"

"We don't know, he hasn't been stung." Lucas said quickly. "Why?"

"Get home now. He got stung and he's having a reaction. We called 9-1-1."

"Shit, we're on our way," Lucas said. "Hey, the neighbor down the street. 1123. His son has a peanut allergy. Get his epi pen."

"On it," Josh said as he ran out the door.

"Stay calm, Zach, help is on the way," she said as she tried to keep his throat open with one hand and stroked his hair with the other. She could hear the ambulance sirens already as Zach struggled to breathe. "You're gonna be okay, buddy. Uncle Josh is on it."

Zach grabbed her hand that was helping him to breath better and lightly held it. She could see panic but also trust in his eyes. She started to quietly sing. "You are my sunshine, my only sunshine…"

Josh ran back into the house to Scout. "Pen."

Right behind him was the neighbor as Scout grabbed the thick gray pen with a blue cap on one

end and an orange cap on the other.
She looked at the neighbor.
"How?"

"Yeah," he said. "Blue to the
sky, orange to the thigh. Take off
the blue cap."

Scout did as he said, then
gripped the pen in the middle and
looked back at him.

"I can do it if you want," he said
quickly.

She shook her head. "I'm good. I
promise."

"Okay," he said. "Drive it into
the middle of his outer thigh, over
his clothes is fine. When it hits his
leg, it'll click. Don't pull back.
Hold it there for five seconds, then
pull it out."

"Got it," she said. Josh came
over and held his leg.

"You got this," he said.

She nodded at Josh as Zach's breathing got even tighter. *Into the thigh, click, hold for five seconds, then pull out.* She nodded.

Josh held his leg as Scout pulled her arm, then *slam!* The needle clicked as soon as it hit Zach's outer thigh and she held it there.

"One…two…three…four…five, " Josh counted.

"And one for good measure," Scout said quietly as she pulled the needle out and put it on the coffee table before looking into Zach's eyes. Immediately his breathing eased, though not completely.

"It'll take five or ten minutes to take full effect," the neighbor said.

"Thank you," Scout said as she scooped Zach into her arms and started quietly singing to him again. He smiled at her as he reached up his hand and touched her face. She couldn't stop the tears that formed as she thanked God he was alive.

"Oh, man, thank you," Josh said as he stood and slapped the neighbor's arm."

"No problem," he replied. "Been there. Done this. Ambulance is here. I'll wave them in."

"Thank you," Josh said. He turned to Scout, and she looked at him with weepy eyes.

"He's okay, baby," he said quietly. He walked over and kissed Zach on the forehead. "You're okay buddy. Mommy and daddy will meet u at the hospital, okay?"

Zach nodded as Josh turned to Casey. "Buddy, we're gonna follow the ambulance, okay?"

"Okay, Uncle Josh," Casey said as he hopped off the couch. He ran over to Zach and kissed his brother on the head. "You'll be okay, buddy."

Zach grinned at his brother as his breathing started to return to normal.

"Come here, Casey, make room," Josh said as the paramedics came in with their equipment.

Scout handed Zach to the medics as she stayed by his side. She was grateful for their quick action and especially for how well she and Josh had worked together. But mostly, she was grateful that Zach was still breathing. It was the

scariest moment of her life, and she
Suddenly knew what it felt like to
be a mother.

13

A Mother's Love

Sirens blared loudly and people rushed in and out of the white swinging doors as Scout rested in the crook of Josh's arm and neck in the busy emergency room. They watched quietly as patients came and went, each one hoping for the best in their given situation. He squeezed her arm and kissed her forehead as they waited for the all-clear.

"You doin' okay?" Josh asked. He gently ran his fingers over her hair.

"I'm okay," she said quietly. "You?"

"I'm okay," he said.

The E.R. doctor who treated Zach when they first arrived had told them the epi pen had probably saved Zach's life.

"Unknown allergies at this age are common," he had said. "We usually see this with bees and food allergies. Especially peanuts and peanut butter."

He had done his best to comfort them and the nurses had gotten a coloring book and crayons for Casey until Lucas and Jaime arrived about an hour later.

"Zach," Jaime had yelled as she ran in with tears with her in eyes. She'd climbed on the bed and scooped him in her arms as Lucas spoke with the doctor. He came in and hugged Casey, then Lucas, before turning to them.

"You saved his life," Lucas had said. "We had no idea he was allergic to bee stings."

"None," Jaime said with tears in her eyes.

"Jaime, they're going to prescribe epi pens for us," Lucas said. "They're going to do some additional allergy testing in a few weeks, too. Just in case."

Jaime had nodded as she held Zach close. Lucas had picked up Casey and held him as he walked to Zach's bed and stroked his hair.

"They're gonna keep you overnight, buddy," Lucas had said.

"We can get your stuff," Josh had offered. "If you wanna stay. We can take Casey."

Jaime had nodded then, and Lucas agreed. "That'd be great," he said. "Give us a second. The doctor's coming back in and then I can tell you what we need, and you can head out. You wanna stay with Uncle Josh?"

"Yes," he said emphatically.

"Awesome," Josh said. "How bout we give you some time. We'll be in the waiting room. Let us know when you're ready."

"Thanks, man," Lucas had said.

And here they'd sat quietly since then.

Scout was wrapped in her thoughts, surprised at the way she felt in this moment. She had always known in her gut she wanted to be a mom. And then they hit this rough patch and she suddenly wasn't sure exactly how much she wanted it given what they'd have to go through. But after this incident, and the way she and Josh had worked together, things had changed.

"I felt like a mom," she said quietly. "A real one."

"You looked like one," Josh whispered. "You were…incredible."

"You were, too," she said. "You looked like a dad."

She pulled away and they smiled at each other.

"What?" Josh asked.

"I want a family, Josh, with you," Scout said. "Just like I said I did. And I'm willing to do what it takes to have it."

"Are you sure?"

"I am. I just wasn't sure about the pathway to it," she said. She shrugged. "I never thought I'd be in the position of not being able to get pregnant. You know?"

"I know. And Scout, I want a family, But not at your expense. So, I'm willing to go as far as you are or not at all, if that's where it ends up," he said. He stroked her hair. "I just want *you*, you know? I love you. You're my family. My whole heart."

She grinned at him. "I know, baby, thank you for saying that."

He nodded at her. "So," he said. "What do you wanna do next?"

She nodded. "I've been thinking about that."

She sighed as she tucked a hair behind her ear. "I'd like to revisit adoption, and I think I'd also like to try the Intrauterine Insemination first."

He smiled as she sighed.

"Josh, I just…I wasn't sure about adoption because I wasn't sure I could love a child that wasn't mine like it was my own," she said. "But, today, with Zach. It just…it just came so naturally. And I knew in that moment, I could love a child, any child, even if it didn't come from us. I could love it like it had."

Josh nodded. "Me, too."

"So, if we can contact the adoption agency and just see where we're at? And then contact the doctor and fertility specialist and get everything ready for the insemination…I think, those are the next steps. What do you think?"

He smiled at her. "Well, you won't believe it when I tell you, but—"

"But, what?" she asked.

"The adoption agency called last week. We've got an interview if you want it."

"Josh," she said as tears hit her eyes. She nodded emphatically. "I want it."

She leapt into his arms as he pulled her close as they both shed a tear or two.

"I'm sorry I didn't tell you sooner," he said. "I just—"

"I get it," she said quietly as she pulled away. She gazed into his eyes, so warm and loving and ready for a family. "It's been hard. For both of us."

He nodded as she smiled at him.

"Let's just get happy for what's next," she said. "And no more tip-toeing around the issue. Sound good?"

"Sounds great," he said.

She slid her hands up her arms as he pulled her into a kiss.

They were finally on the same page and ready to walk into their future together.

14

The Interview

Josh shifted nervously in the worn, stained office chair as he loosened the knot of his tie. He silently wished he hadn't worn something so formal as he smiled easily at the young, blonde in front of him. Clara. Her name was Clara. All he could do at this point was hope for the best as the teenager eyed him fumbling with his blue silk.

"I really liked your profile," she said. She shrugged as she snapped her gum, then glanced at her cell phone.

Josh peered at Scout who raised a sculpted eyebrow. She noisily

cleared her throat and the girl
looked back up at them.

"Sorry," she said as she put the
phone down. "So, you're in
fashion?"

Scout nodded as she put her
coffee cup down on the tattered
office table in front of them. The
Sunshine adoption offices were not
nearly as sunny as the caseworkers
who helped bring families together,
but they got the job done.

"I run Double Digits," Scout
said. She shifted in her seat. Scout
had spent three hours trying to find
the right dress to wear. She'd
modeled at least twelve dresses for
him before landing on this long,
Kelly green sundress number. She
said it looked "maternal." But Josh
doubted that any outfit would have

won this doe-eyed sixteen-year-old over. It seemed as though her mind was made up and it wasn't them.

"Yeah, fire," Clara said off-handedly. "I love Scout's Honor. She's an amazing designer. She has her own television show now, did you see?"

"We helped facilitate it," Scout said.

"No way, you know her personally?"

Josh could see they finally tapped into something Clara was interested in. Maybe this could turn the tide?

"Yeah, we do," Scout said. "But we'd rather get to know you a little better. So, you go to a high school in Wheeling? West Virginia?"

"Yeah." She picked up her phone again. "Cheerleader."

"Do you mind if we ask about the father?" Scout pressed.

"No, that's okay." Clara scrolled through her phone, stopped and clicked, then turned the phone to them, showing them a picture. "That's him."

Scout and Josh leaned in to see the athletic, young, Hispanic man.

"He play sports?" Josh asked.

"Soccer."

"He a nice guy?" Josh continued.

She shrugged. "He's not mean."

"Okay," he said quietly. He glanced at Scout. What the hell was he supposed to do with that comment?

"Uh, and what about you?"
Scout asked picking up the slack in
the conversation. "What do you
like to do besides cheerleading?"

"I like to swim. And I'm a
lifeguard in the summers," she said.
She shifted in her seat like she was
annoyed. "My dad thinks I've
ruined my life."

"Oh, no, I wouldn't say that at
all," Scout said. She shook her head
emphatically.

"I agree," Josh said. "I see kids
at the Foundation all the time who
run into unexpected twists and
turns in their lives. They always
find a way."

Clara nodded as she glanced at
her phone, then put it down. "I
wanted to keep it at first."

Scout and Josh nodded.

"Makes sense," Scout said.

"But, like, I wanna go to college. And…well, he's not my boyfriend. It was just a stupid little thing, you know. One time. I still can't believe it."

Clara glanced at her fingers as she twiddled them.

"My fingers are fat now," she said. "My ankles, too."

Josh reached over and squeezed Scout's knee. She glanced at him and they gave each other weak smiles.

"Clara, you're gonna be okay," Scout said. "No matter what. It's all going to turn out exactly as it should.

Mandy smiled as she sat up a little straighter and quieted her hands.

"You think?" she asked.

"Yeah," Scout said as Josh nodded in agreement.

"Do you mind if we ask, why did you pick us to interview?" Josh questioned.

"Uh, you both had jobs. Good ones. My parents said that was important," she quipped. "And I thought you kind of looked like the dad with your dark hair and eyes."

She nodded at Josh as he smiled. "I see," he said.

"I also liked that you both love to travel," Clara said quietly. "I'm not ever gonna get out of that town. But I want her to."

"It's a girl?" Scout said as tears rushed her eyes.

Clara nodded with a smile.

Scout reached down and squeezed Josh's hand still on her leg.

"But I didn't name her or anything," Clara said. "They said you shouldn't do that. You know. So, you don't get attached."

Scout nodded as she wiped her eyes.

"How are we doing in here?" the Sunshine counselor Brenda said as she walked in and sat down. Her voice was light and airy.

"Good," Josh said. He eyed Brenda. He recognized her dress pants. They were from last year's spring line and she looked great in them. The woman had style.

"Yeah," Scout agreed. "We're doing great."

Clara just smiled and Josh didn't think that was a good sign either. They hadn't done anything wrong but Brenda had warned them the process could hit or miss and not to take it personally.

"Okay, well, if there aren't any more questions, Clara is going to think about this, and we'll let you know sometime in the next week or so what she decides. Sound good?"

"Sounds good," Josh said. He and Scout stood up and shook Brenda's hand.

"Good to see you again," he said.

"You, too, Josh," she said warmly. "And you Scout."

Josh turned to Clara and shook her hand, too, though it seemed she'd much rather have gone to a

dentist appointment. Typical
teenager stuff, though her situation
was not. He had to imagine this
was difficult for her to deal with,
too.

"We wish you the very best,
Clara," Josh said. "We know it's
not easy."

"Thanks," she said. And he got a
genuine smile from her.

"Yeah, and let us know if you
have any more questions," Scout
added as she came up and shook
her hand, too.

"Okay, thank you," Mandy said.
She let go of Scout's hand and
shrugged. "I appreciate it."

Scout and Josh waved once more
to Brenda then walked out of the
office and the building to her
Lexus. As they got in and put their

seatbelts on Josh sat back and looked at Scout.

"Well, what do you think?" Josh asked.

Now it was Scout's turn to shrug. "I'm not sure," she said. "But I have a feeling, it's not our baby, Josh."

"Yeah," he said as he started the engine. "I got that impression, too."

"I guess my dress didn't matter, did it?"

He peered at her and saw the sadness cross her beautiful face. He leaned over and touched her face, then pulled her to him and gave her a light kiss.

"Remember what Brenda said. We can't take these personally."

He saw a rush of tears to her eyes, and it made his insides hurt. It

was hard on him, sure, but it wasn't
nearly as hard as it was on Scout.

"It's gonna be okay, baby," he
whispered.

"I know," she squeaked out.

"How about I take you to dinner,
huh?"

"Can we just get Chinese and go
home? Eat on the patio?"

"Sure, babe, let's do it."

"The same place we got Chinese
food that first time. In Pappy's
office. Remember?"

She turned a smile in his
direction, and it lit him up inside.
That had been their first dinner
together and it had been perfect—
until Lucas had interrupted.

"I remember," he said. "Let's do
it."

"Okay," she said quietly as she wiped her face dry.

"Okay," he said. "Then we can take a walk around the property with Buster? Check out where we want to put some new flowers next spring?"

"I'd like that." She smiled as he pulled out of the parking lot. Maybe all they needed was a little night air, the romance of twilight, and time to make this all start feeling better.

15

Under the Starry Sky

Scout sighed from the fullness of a delicious Pad Thai dinner and a lovely evening with Josh as they walked hand-in-hand around their massive property making a checklist of what to remove and what to add. Buster was happy, too, and tired from all the walking as they arrived back at the house and landed on their wraparound front porch.

"Come on, Buster," Josh said as the pooped pooch gladly went inside for water and his doggy bed. "He's beat."

"Good. He'll sleep later," she said. She smiled as she leaned against the porch post and watched her sexy husband stroll up to her. "You look good, baby."

"Thank you," he said. He leaned in and kissed her lightly as she slid her hands up his arms and breathed him in. He always smelled good, even when he wasn't wearing cologne. It was just his natural scent mixed with notes of soap, shampoo, and shaving cream. He peered at her with those deep, dark eyes as twilight took hold and the stars popped out. He slid his hands around her waist, and it made butterflies dance in her belly with anticipation. He had that look in his eyes, the seductive one. He squeezed her backside and nodded to the pond.

"New flowers coming up," he said with a wink.

"I see that," she replied. A slight grin touched her lips.

"Wanna take a lap and talk for a minute?"

She nodded. She wasn't sure what his plan was, but she liked it already. He was always surprising her with fun and sexy things. And she loved that he loved her fiercely and always, no matter what. She could see that in R.J., too, but she suspected a lot of how he treated her came from his relationship with his mother.

She noticed the gentle movement of the pond water from the breeze as they approached it and how the lights on the pond's short dock gave it a pretty glow in the coming darkness. She had an inkling his mother would have loved the way it had all come together across the property, from the flowers and the trees to the gazebo on the west side of the property and this lighted dock.

"How often did you and your mom come down here?"

"A lot," Josh said. "But right before she died was the first and only time we painted here."

"She was a good mom, huh?"

"The best," Josh said. "She did the usual stuff, you know, like cut the crust off our peanut butter sandwiches and give us band-aids when we didn't need them just because they had Batman on them. She read us bedtime stories. But then she did different things like learning how to ice skate so she could help us with hockey and

sleeping in tents under the stars
with an endless supply of hot
chocolate."

"That sounds lovely," Scout said
wistfully.

"It really was," Josh said. He
smiled. "What about your mom?"

"You know most of it already. I
mean, my parents aren't super
touchy-feely," Scout said. "But as a
child, my mom was always there,
and she was always on my side.
Like, there was this bully at school
one time who kept trying to take
my lunch money and my mom
fought with the school and the
other mom until it stopped."

Josh laughed. "Sounds like
something your mom would do."

"Yeah, she didn't hug me a lot,
but she loved me," Scout said. "I

want to be fierce like that. But I also want to be loving, like your mom. You know, touchy-feely. I'm worried I won't be."

"You will, Scout," Josh said. "I've watched you with Zach and Casey. You hug and love those two all the time."

"You think?" she asked.

"I do," he responded. He pulled her to him and slid his hands under her chin, tilting her face up to his. He kissed her deeply as the crickets chirped loudly.

"Mmm," she moaned as she slid her hands up his back and kissed him back.

"I need you, Josh," she whispered.

"Mmm, I need you, too," he said. He picked her up and carried her to the porch, where he put her down and gently moved her up against the railings. He reached down and slid her green dress up over her hips as she carefully leaned back on the railing bar and balanced her weight with her hands.

"Yes, baby," she said seductively.

He unbuckled his belt and pants and let them drop as she reached her hand to him and massaged his manhood. He let out a groan and took her lips in his.

"I love you so much, baby," she said as he pulled his head back and stepped between her legs. He grabbed her bare thighs as she wrapped them around his waist, then she slid her hands around his neck and pulled him close.

"I love you, too," he replied. "So much, Scout."

He slid his hands around her waist as they made love under the starry sky. They didn't think about anything else for the rest of the night except how much they loved each other.

And it was exactly the release they both needed.

16

The Hardest No to Hear

A week later, Josh grinned playfully at his smoking hot wife and her curvaceous body as she walked to the breakfast table with pleasure written all over her face. Since their starry night escapade, they'd made love every single day and had reconnected in ways they hadn't before. They were finally in the same place together and moving forward toward the same goal each with a much deeper understanding of the other.

"Damn, baby, you're gorgeous," he said as he slapped her cute little bottom.

"Josh, stop," she giggled. She cast a cute glance at him. "Do it again."

He laughed as he gave her another playful slap and she got her coffee with Buster in tow.

"The fertility specialist called about a half hour ago," Josh said. "Come here, Buster."

He petted the happy dog whose tail was on full wag mode.

"Oh, that's who was on the phone?" she asked as she poured a little cream in the rich, dark Brazilian blend.

"Yep. And they want to do the procedure after Thanksgiving," Josh said. "Does that work for you?"

She nodded. "Yeah, that works. It'll be nice to just focus on the holidays and come back to it after."

"Agreed," he said. "Lay down, Buster."

As the dog laid down by their feet, he walked to his wife as she sipped her coffee. Even just standing in the kitchen with her messy hair and no make-up, she was the most alluring woman he'd ever seen. "Your parents are flying in the day before?"

"They are, so full house," she quipped.

"I'm so excited to host our first Thanksgiving," Josh said.

"Me, too. Can't wait to put our tree up." She walked over and kissed him. "I'm gonna hop in the shower."

"Wait," he said as he picked up
his vibrating phone. "It's the
adoption agency."

"Oh," she said. She walked back
as Josh put the phone down on the
counter and hit the speaker button.

"This is Josh," he said.

"Hi Josh, Brenda here," she said.

"Hey there," he said. "Scout is
also here. You're on speaker
phone."

"Oh good," she said. "Hi Scout."

"Hey Brenda," Scout replied.
She gripped her coffee.

"Listen, I wish I had better news,
especially right before the holidays,
and you two are so amazing, but
unfortunately, Clara picked the
other family for her baby."

Scout's eyes misted over as she
nodded to Josh and put her coffee

down. They had suspected as much, but it didn't make it any easier to hear. He walked to his wife, kissed her, and pulled her into his body as he rubbed her back.

"We understand," Josh said. He kissed the top of Scout's head as he held her tight. She pulled back and squeezed him, giving him a kiss, then turning toward the phone.

"Do you mind if I ask, why?"

"Well, it was a couple reasons. The other couple looked a little more like the birth mother and father. That was a big thing for Clara," Brenda said.

"Yeah, she had mentioned that to me, too, when we interviewed with her," Josh noted.

"Right," Brenda agreed. "The other thing was that the second

family is much further away.
They're over on the east coast. And
I think Clara had some concerns
about being too close to the baby."

"Gotcha," Scout said. "I can
understand that."

"She really liked you both,"
Brenda said brightly. "But I think
the distance and the looks were
most important to her right now."

"Sure, we get it," Scout said.

"Yeah, we do," Josh said quietly.
"The birth mom has to be
comfortable for her reasons. We
understand."

"Right," Brenda agreed. "The
big question moving forward is, do
you want us to keep you on the list
for a baby?"

Josh and Scout smiled at each other as he rubbed her arms. "What do you want?" he whispered.

"More time," she whispered back. He nodded.

"Can we talk about that and get back to you?" Josh asked. "We're about to go through a fertility treatment and I think we just need some time."

"Sure thing," Brenda replied. "How about you get back to me after the New Year. Sound good?"

"Yeah," Scout and Josh said at the same time.

"Great, I'll look forward to it," she said. "You two have a good day. And a great holiday break."

"Thank you, you, too, Brenda," Josh said.

"Yes, thank you, Brenda," Scout added. Josh hung up and looked into Scout's jade-colored eyes. In the past, they would have been stormy with defeat. But now, they were bright with hope.

"I think we'll have a better grasp of what we want after we get through the holidays," Scout said.

"Yeah, I think so, too," Josh said.

"Until then, I need to shower, and you need to go get our turkey," she said. She headed out of the kitchen as Josh happily watched her sexy little body bounce away.

"Don't forget to get the Christmas lights out of the basement," she yelled over her shoulder as she disappeared.

"Consider it done," he yelled back.

They both had hope that the insemination procedure would work, and they wouldn't need to do anything else after that. But if it was up to Josh, he'd adopt and he'd have one of his own if that was in the cards for them. After all the work he'd done at the Foundation and the kids they'd helped, plus meeting Clara, he knew there were children who needed good homes.

And he and Scout had a good home and so much love to give, it just made sense in his mind to give that to a child who really needed it. Needed them.

But first things first. Get through the holidays and figure it all out later. He poured out Scout's half-full coffee cup into the sink and grinned at Buster.

"Wanna help me put Christmas lights up, buddy?"

Buster sighed and dropped his head down to paws, looking away.

"Chump," Josh said. He laughed as he headed to the basement to get the holiday decorations. Christmas was their special time of year and it always had been. And he wanted to make this one the best they'd had ever had.

17

Thanksgiving Dinner

Scout had woken up to the delicious smell of the roasting turkey wafting through the house and immediately jumped out of bed and threw up. She was absolutely certain she had the flu. It had been going around the company and she had done everything to avoid it, from wearing a mask in meetings to rubbing sanitizer gel all over her hands every five minutes. And now, here she was, lying in bed, queasy and iffy on Thanksgiving Day, her favorite holiday, and the whole family was coming.

"Baby, do you want me to get you a ginger ale?" Josh asked from the bedroom door. He was sexy as ever, in basic blue jeans, a navy-blue polo, and barefoot. She, on the other hand was wearing no make-up, hair in a bun, and wearing a tank top and silk pajama pants as Buster cuddled next to her.

"No," she said. She patted Buster's head. "Just give me a minute. I'm moving."

"But if you have the flu, we don't want to get anyone else sick."

"I know, I know," she said. "But it's Thanksgiving. I'll wear a mask. Maybe it's just a 24-hour bug and it'll go away."

"Well, let's hope so," he said. He leaned back against the door frame and grinned at her. "I'm just bummed you might not be able to eat my amazing turkey. I knocked this meal out of the park, baby."

"Hey, I helped," she said as she gingerly climbed out of bed followed by Buster, who made his way to Josh. She carefully stood and started to make her way to the bathroom. "I made the rolls."

"You bought the rolls," he corrected.

"Same difference."

"Sure, baby, whatever you say." They both chuckled as the doorbell rang. "Doh, that's Lucas and Jaime and the kids. You need anything?"

"Nope," she hollered from the bathroom as she walked into the cool, comforting space. This bathroom was one of her favorite rooms in the house. Peaceful and calm like a spa. "Just, are my parents up?"

"Yep. And I already made them breakfast," he yelled from the bedroom door. "They've got the parade on."

"Perfect." She leaned against the sink.

"Okay, holler if you need anything. Or text me." She heard him rush down the stairway and swing open the door. The excited tones of family arriving made her smile as she glanced in the mirror at her reflection.

"Yuck." She pulled on her bun and looked at her tired eyes.

She couldn't believe her dumb luck, getting sick on Thanksgiving, when everyone was gathering in their home for the first time they'd hosted. She lumped over the sink as her stomach turned.

"Ugh," she uttered. All she could do was hope that whatever this was, it would ease up in time for dinner.

Scout took another bite of pumpkin pie drenched in whipped cream and was glad her bug had cleared up long enough to eat Thanksgiving food, minus the turkey for some reason.

"This was delicious, Josh," Scout's mother, Helene, said.

"Agreed," added Katherine. "Five stars to the chef."

"Here, here," Lucas said as he raised his glass. Everyone obliged and cheered him.

"I had a good assistant," Josh said. He leaned over and kissed Scout as he gave her a private wink.

"The rolls were delicious." Scout laughed. "I know you all loved them."

"Yes, honey good job buying the best ones in the store," said Scout's father, Luis.

"Here, here," Jaime said teasingly. Another round of cheers followed as they all laughed.

"Alright, should we clean up then play some euchre?" Josh asked. He slapped his hands together.

"Let's do it," Lucas said. "Ladies, we've got this. Dad."

"Damn it, why are you two dragging me into this?" R.J. huffed. "Football!"

"Later," Josh said. "This won't take any time at all. Come on old man."

"I'll help, too," Luis said as he stood up and started clearing the plates.

The women laughed as Casey and Zach played with their iPads and Buster tried to lick the leftovers off their faces and hands.

"Buster, lay down," Scout laughed as the dog obeyed and laid down with the kids.

"Fantastic meal," Katherine said. She leaned back in her chair and patted her stomach.

"Let's talk important stuff," Jaime said with a grin. She rubbed her stomach, which was protruding now with the growing baby. Scout thought Jaime was one of the most beautiful pregnant women she'd ever seen. A natural, certainly, and easy going about everything. "What time are we shopping tomorrow?"

"Early," Helene said. "As long as you're not sick again, honey." She reached over and patted Scout's hand. Scout grabbed her mother's hand and squeezed it confidently.

"I should be okay," Scout replied.

"Sick? What was wrong?" Katherine asked. She sat up and leaned forward toward Scout.

"I think I'm fighting off the flu," Scout said. "Or maybe a little twenty-four-hour bug or something."

The ladies all looked at each other, then back to Scout.

"You sure about that?" Jaime asked cautiously.

"What do you mean?" Scout's brow furrowed. She looked at all the faces staring back at her. "What? The flu's been going around the company."

"You know what, that's probably it. Let's drop it, huh? I've got a shopping list to make anyway," Helene said. "Scout, I'm starting with you. What do you and Josh want this year?"

As the ladies went back and forth about what presents to get for whom and how the gift exchange was going to work, Scout peered at

the women and wondered happily
to herself about her unexpected
illness.

Maybe, just maybe, she
wondered, it wasn't the flu after all.

18

Black Friday

Scout sat down in the dressing room of Nordstrom's as the Christmas music blared loudly on Black Friday. She told the ladies she was coming to try on a dress, but in reality she needed to sit down and catch her breath. The nausea was back and this time it was overwhelming.

"You okay, Scout?" Jaime asked from just outside the door as she knocked lightly.

"Yeah, fine," Scout said weakly. "Thanks for asking."

Scout covered her mouth as the sickness ran the length of her body. This was definitely not the flu. She had no fever and she'd only been getting sick in the mornings and early afternoons. By dinner, she was fine and able to eat—everything except chicken and turkey.

But, somehow, in between the moments of wanting to puke, Scout had spent her time grinning widely from ear-to-ear. The possibility that she was pregnant had hit her last night after Thanksgiving dinner when she and the ladies were talking. And then again, while she and Josh were having sex later.

The doctor had told them time and again that getting pregnant wasn't impossible, just difficult. And as Josh had moved inside her, she had thought back a month or so to the that steamy shower sex they'd had, when they both had relaxed and just loved each other instead of trying to force a pregnancy. It must have happened then. That was the timeframe and the situation that made the most sense.

She laughed as a sleeve of Saltine crackers came flying under the door. She grabbed it, then opened the dressing room door as Jaime rushed in.

"Oh my God," Jaime said as she started to jump up and down and Scout laughed.

"Shhh," Scout said. "Please don't' say anything. I don't know."

"But you think?" Jaime said quietly holding back her excitement.

Scout nodded emphatically and they both started jumping again.

"Okay, I have a plan," Jaime said.

"Of course you do," Scout said with a roll of her eyes.

"I'll distract the moms, you run across the street to the drugstore and grab a pregnancy test, then hit the mall bathroom and come back when you're done."

"That's a super covert operation," Scout said.

"It is. And you have to go right now while they're in the dressing rooms."

"Okay," Scout said excitedly. She grabbed her purse and they both opened the door and peeked out. Jaime shoved her.

"Go!"

Scout listened to her sister-in-law and ran for the exit. She ran out

the mall, across the street, and into
the drug store. She scanned the
pregnancy tests.

"Holy shit, how many are there
now?" she whispered. She grabbed
four of them and checked out at the
self-check-out station, ran back
across the street, into the mall, and
to the bathrooms. She ran to the
first open stall available and locked
herself inside, hanging up her purse
on the hook.

Scout excitedly opened up all
four of the tests and carefully set
them on the toilet paper holder as
she sat down on the toilet and
prepared herself. She quickly and
efficiently peed on every single
one, set them up, and then pulled
up her jeans. She grabbed hand
sanitizer and cleaned herself up,

then set her timer on her phone and waited. She leaned her back against the tiny, metal stall wall as women came in and went out to the tune of flushing toilets and hand-drying blowers.

This was it. She couldn't believe it. Neither she nor Josh expected to get pregnant without medical intervention. If she was, in fact, pregnant, it was a miracle. And that was pure joy and happiness. It also made her sad for all the women who didn't get to have this moment. Or had to go through hell to get it. She let out a grateful sigh as the timer went off.

Ad now she was scared to look. Scared it was negative. Maybe she'd thought happy thoughts too soon? And she wasn't going to

have the family she so desperately
wanted with Josh. Then she was
scared it was positive. What if she
got everything she ever wanted,
and it wasn't enough? She shook
her head at her scattered thoughts.
She was just nervous.

She took a deep breath, closed
her eyes, and exhaled. She took a
step away from the wall and tilted
her head down at the tests, then
opened her eyes.

Tears immediately gathered and
fell down her cheeks as the first
thought that crossed her mind was,
"Josh."

19

I Love You

Josh could smell the pot roast the minute he walked through the door. Scout was a good cook; she just didn't usually have time for it. And besides, he liked running the kitchen. Cooking was his favorite pastime and maybe, someday, he was considering opening a restaurant.

He was starting to grasp the concept that he enjoyed being a serial entrepreneur. First his photo gallery, next a restaurant, and who knew what after that? But for tonight, his baby was cooking, and he was excited. Her pot roast and vegetables were five stars all the way.

"Baby?" he yelled. "Are you home?"

"Kitchen," Scout yelled.

Scout being home early was new, too.

"What the hell is going on?" he whispered. He dropped his bag on the side table and hung his keys on the rack by the door. He gave Buster a hearty hello, then walked into the kitchen. Scout was a sight for sore eyes, dressed in a skimpy little outfit with her hair loose around her face.

"Fuck, baby, you're sexy," he said. He rushed over to her and pulled her into him letting her feel how turned on he was.

"Oh baby" she said. "What's that?"

"You know what that is," he said deeply. "What's gotten into you? Home early, cooking, sexy as all hell."

He kissed her deeply as she returned the favor, sliding her hands up his back and writhing against him.

"Baby, damn," he breathed. She started to undress him, and it was game on. He wasn't sure what was going on but he didn't care. Surprises like this were meant for enjoying, not questioning. "Fuck yes."

They stripped each other of all their clothes and dropped to the kitchen floor as he positioned himself between her legs and she pulled him urgently toward her.

"Josh, yes," she panted.

"Holy shit, baby, yes," he
groaned. He slid inside her as they
reached unbelievable heights of
passion right there on the kitchen
floor, as the warmth of their
kitchen, and the smell of their
dinner filled the air.

Josh laughed as he looked over
at Scout on the floor.

"Baby, wow," he said. "What
was that for?"

She laughed. "Because I love
you, that's why."

"Oh yeah?"

"Yeah," she said. She cuddled
into his shoulder as she ran her
finger up and down his chest. He

returned the favor, running his fingers up and down her back.

"I could do that every day. I don't even need dinner."

"Oh yes you do, I worked hard on it," she said.

He laughed. "Seriously, is everything okay?"

"Better than okay," she said quietly.

"Scout?" he asked as he glanced down at his wife, and she smiled up at him. He knew that look of happiness. Knew his wife. And suddenly his heart jumped with an understanding and unexpected joy. No, it couldn't be.

He sat straight up, bringing her with him. "Scout? Are you…?"

The smile on her face and tears in her eyes told him everything he needed to know. Of course, it all made sense now. The sickness at Thanksgiving, her aversion to meat, the dinner and her being home early to talk. And now, that look in her beautiful green eyes as she gazed at him.

He was going to be a father.

"Scout." He pulled her in close and held on tight. He was so grateful for her and for their future family. There were absolutely no words. Well, that was wrong. There were three: "I love you."

20

Holiday Party

Josh knew he was beaming from the inside-out as their families swirled around them drinking eggnog and holiday cocktails at R.J. and Katherine's house. The food was delicious. R.J. had catered in a feast fit for royalty, so no one had to lift a finger for their holiday celebration. Josh figured it was so no one could force him on dish duty like Thanksgiving.

Josh smiled to himself as he watched Casey and Zach run around from the desserts sugar high. They were playing cops and robbers just like him and Lucas used to do. R.J. and Katherine danced to the Christmas music in their own little world. Jaime sat on Lucas' lap as he rubbed her belly and laughed. Helene and Luis were fussing with the Christmas presents and putting them into piles. It was noisy and messy and perfect.

"It's almost time," Scout whispered as she sauntered up to him. She was right. It was almost time to open presents and he and Scout had carefully prepared special gifts for each of their parents. He kissed her gently and touched her stomach.

"You feelin' okay?" he asked quietly.

"A little nauseated from the ham but I'm good," she said. She shrugged with happiness. "I can't wait to see their faces."

"Me, too," he said.

As if on cue, the music transitioned to a new song and R.J. yelled, "It's present time!" Everyone gathered quickly around the tree, picking their sitting spot to enjoy the festivities.

"Yay!" Casey yelled as he grabbed Zach and pulled him right to the front of the glittering pine.

"Kids first," Katherine yelled.

"Not this year," Josh interrupted.

"What?" R.J. said surprised. Everyone turned to him as he grabbed Scout's hand and squeezed.

"We actually have a present for the parents we want to do first," Josh said.

Scout turned and grabbed four small bags from behind the tree.

She handed one to each of their parents.

"What is this, Scout?" her mother asked.

"Yeah, what is this, sweetie?" Luis asked as he took the bag from his daughter.

"You'll see," she teased. She kissed his cheek. "Merry Christmas."

"Merry Christmas," Josh added.

The parents looked at each other, then excitedly tore into their bags. It was R.J. who reacted first, as though he knew what it was and had been waiting for it.

"Hot damn!" he yelled as he pulled out the onesie that read, *I'm Papaw's favorite.* "Another baby!"

A chorus of yells erupted from the parents as they swarmed Josh

and Scout and hugged them
emphatically, then each other, then
Scout.

"A grandbaby!" Helene
exclaimed as she pulled her
daughter into a hug. "You are going
to be an amazing mother."

"Yes, you are," Katherine added
as she swooped in on the hug.

"Why aren't you two surprised?"
R.J. asked as he glanced at Lucas
and Jaime.

"Oh, well—"

"Let me guess, you two
schemers knew already?"
Katherine interrupted sarcastically.

Jaime and Lucas grinned.

"A pregnant mom knows another
pregnant mom when she sees her,"
Jaime said as she pointed at Scout.

"Yes, she does," Scout said happily with a nod to Jaime.

"No matter." R.J. grabbed his glass and raised it, as everyone quickly followed suit.

"I have something I want to say," R.J. said. Everyone quieted down as the patriarch spoke. "All those years ago, Paps and Bessie had a dream for a family. A big one. A happy one. And everything they did was for that dream. And here we all are today, a continuation of that dream for family and everything it means. I am so grateful for that dream. And for all of you. Congratulations, Josh and Scout. Salute!"

A chorus of salutes filled the air as they each sipped their drinks.

"Presents!" Casey yelled impatiently.

"Yes, presents," Katherine said back excitedly.

As they all worked to get the kids their presents, Scout pulled Josh aside.

"Josh, I've been thinking."

"Yeah?" he asked quietly.

"Meeting Clara…that really hit me," she said.

"Yeah, me too."

"I think…I think I'd like to adopt a baby and go back on the list," she said. "We have so much love to give. And what your dad just said…I want a big family. And I want to give that to a child who needs someone to love them."

Josh smiled broadly. "I want that, too. You know how much it means to me because of my work with the Foundation."

"I do," she said. She grinned.

"So, we go back on the list?" he asked.

"We go back on the list," she said.

"Scout, I love you," Josh said. "So much."

"Me, too, baby," she said. "Me, too."

As the kids shouted with joy in the background, Josh kissed Scout and knew he had everything he could ever want.

21

Possibilities

One year later

Josh shuffled through the sea of pink outfits that filled the drawers of the nursery dresser as he searched for one very specific onesie that he couldn't seem to find.

"Scout!" he yelled. "Where's the onesie?"

"Which onesie?" she yelled back.

"You know the one," he yelled as he shut the drawer and peered into his daughter's green eyes on the changing station. "Mommy knows where it's at, I'm telling you, kid."

She grinned as she kicked her tiny pink arms and legs.

"Am I reading minds now, is that the new thing?" Scout said as she walked into the nursery.

"I mean, yeah, we're married. Comes with the territory, right?" he asked teasingly.

She laughed as she grabbed the laundry basket, sorted through it, and pulled out the pink, "Daddy is #1" onesie with little white flowers all over it. "Seriously, Josh?"

He grinned. "The laundry basket is where I was headed next."

"For a stay-at-home dad running multiple businesses and with mad organizational skills, I'm surprised you had that much trouble finding it."

"Hey," he said as he took the onesie from her and dressed their smiling daughter. "I just started a month ago. I'm still adjusting. Plus, I wanted to see my sexy wife."

She sauntered up to him and gave him a sweet kiss.

"You miss being full-time at the Foundation?" she asked.

"Yeah, I do, but serving on the board helps." He picked up his sweet girl and held her close.

"I bet," she said.

"You're doing amazing with the company, baby. Glad to be back after maternity leave?"

"Love it," she said. "But I miss you, Anastasia."

Scout took the little angle from him and grinned at Josh. "You think this time it's going to be the right one?"

"I guess we'll find out," he said. He straightened his clothes. This time, it was a simple polo and basic dress pants. And for Scout, a simple white dress with sandals. "You look great."

"Thanks, you, too," she said. She looked at Anastasia. "You, too, sweetie."

Scout loved and kissed her daughter as Josh wrapped his arms around them both and kissed Scout. "I love you."

"I love you, too," she said.

"Alright, let's go see if this baby is our baby." This time, Josh felt certain they were the family the adoptive mother was looking for. They'd had one phone interview

already, and now the in-person
interview at the Sunshine agency.
All signs had been good and
pointing toward them, though they
were trying not to get too far ahead
of themselves this time.

As Scout bounced Anastasia in
her arms, she said, "You know, I
have the strangest feeling this baby
is ours, Josh."

"Yeah," Josh said. He smiled.
"Me, too."

He gave Scout a kiss, then she
turned and walked out the door
with their beautiful daughter. There
was never a day that went by that
Josh didn't think about Paps and
that day all those years ago when
his grandfather had brought up
Scout's name and gave Josh a look
with a devilish twinkle in his eye.

Paps had known. It was his grandfather who had first seen that Scout was the perfect person for Josh. That Josh was more than just Double Digits. That Scout was the woman to lead the family company, and Josh needed to find his own way.

R.J.'s Christmas toast a year ago had been spot on—Paps had started this family with his lifelong love, Bessie. And R.J. had carried it on with Josh's mother, and then Katherine. And now, Josh and Lucas had brought everything full circle.

This was their family. For better and worse. And he couldn't wait to see what came next for them.

He glanced at the heavens and grinned.

"Love you, Paps." He let out an exhale. "Tell grandma and mom I said hello."

With that, he grabbed Anastasia's diaper bag and walked out the door.